"I WANT TO KNOW WHY YOU'VE BEEN SNEAKING AROUND BEHIND MY BACK!" DEVIN DEMANDED.

"What ever do you mean?" Bonnie asked innocently.

"Don't goad me! You *know* what I mean!"

"If you're referring to my pleasant lunch with your daughter, I'd hardly call that sneaking behind your back. She's an adult and perfectly free to choose her friends."

"Is that what you are?" he asked coolly.

"No, I read her palm and told her fortune with chicken bones," she said flippantly.

"I wouldn't put it past you."

"Your delusions are your problem," she shot back. "We ate, talked . . . you know, held a normal conversation of the kind you and I seem incapable of for more than a few minutes at a time lately. Does that answer your question?"

"Hardly. But coming from you, what else can I expect? With you everything is always a mystery."

"No, Devin, never a mystery. Just magic."

CANDLELIGHT ECSTASY ROMANCES®

MAGIC TOUCH

Linda Vail

A CANDLELIGHT ECSTASY ROMANCE®

Published by
Dell Publishing Co., Inc.
1 Dag Hammarskjold Plaza
New York, New York 10017

Dell ® TM 681510, Dell Publishing Co., Inc.

Candlelight Ecstasy Romance®, 1,203,540, is a registered
trademark of Dell Publishing Co., Inc., New York, New York.

ISBN: 0-440-15173-2

Printed in the United States of America
First printing—March 1985

To Our Readers:

We have been delighted with your enthusiastic response to Candlelight Ecstasy Romances®, and we thank you for the interest you have shown in this exciting series.

In the upcoming months we will continue to present the distinctive sensuous love stories you have come to expect only from Ecstasy. We look forward to bringing you many more books from your favorite authors and also the very finest work from new authors of contemporary romantic fiction.

As always, we are striving to present the unique, absorbing love stories that you enjoy most—books that are more than ordinary romance. Your suggestions and comments are always welcome. Please write to us at the address below.

Sincerely,

The Editors
Candlelight Romances
1 Dag Hammarskjold Plaza
New York, New York 10017

CHAPTER ONE

Anyone observing Dr. Devin Warner would only have supposed him mildly annoyed, with his slight frown, the hint of distaste etched on his chiseled features, and the obvious disbelief in his arctic-blue eyes. And usually he would have been observed, for eyes—especially female eyes—were often drawn to this conservatively dressed man with the healthy head of auburn hair.

But very few if any eyes, of any gender, were on him at the moment. Everyone was watching the ghostly apparition who had made the aisle of the children's ward her center stage. And Devin was not annoyed. He was entranced.

She was dressed in white—a loose, billowing silk blouse and pants—with an emerald-colored sash around her trim waist. The same shade of green as her eyes, Devin noted, wondering why he should be paying so much attention. She was only a magician, come to entertain the children. It disturbed him to realize that she was entertaining him as well.

He was a scientist, a realist, an extraordinarily gifted eye surgeon and research physician. He was much too busy for such foolishness. Still, there was something about her . . .

With a hypnotizing swirl of her waist-length red hair, Bonnie Tyson turned and showed her attentive young audience her hands; the long, graceful fingers held bright red spheres between each fingertip. She moved her hands only slightly, and eight balls became six, then four. With a flourish and a toss of that magnificent red mane, she spun again and showed the awestruck children empty hands, looking quite astonished herself. It was only simple sleight of hand, but it pleased both her and the children.

For a moment the hospital ward was silent. Then came a collective gasp, then applause and excited chatter. Bonnie looked from face to face and smiled broadly. "Magic!" she said in an audible whisper. She went to the corridor behind her to fetch a trunk, which she then pulled to the center of the room, positioning it so all the children could see.

Devin convinced himself he only wanted to see the illusion she was about to perform, but he knew it was her smooth, fluid movements that had drawn him deeper into the room. He was six feet tall himself and judged the lady magician to be at least a foot shorter. Yet her every movement seemed to convey a feeling of power. Was he imagining it, or had she looked at him for a moment, her eyes at once childlike and womanly? He shook his head in doubt, but he watched.

Bonnie opened the trunk and showed that it was empty. Then she closed it and spun it around twice, stopping to look up expectantly. "I need an assistant!" she declared.

Several willing hands popped up, accompanied by compelling cries of "Me! Me!"

"No, no," Bonnie said with a wave of her hand, the loose sleeve of her blouse flapping dramatically. "You're all too willing. I need someone who doesn't believe in magic!" Immediately the small hands went down. They were obviously all believers. For a second time the emerald gaze went to the handsome doctor in the white lab coat who stood in the corner. She could see the doubt in his eyes. "Doctor . . ." Her voice trailed off, thus completing the question as she waved him over.

Devin reluctantly complied. "Warner," he answered.

"Do you believe in magic, Dr. Warner?"

"No," he replied flatly.

Bonnie's brow furrowed for a moment, but her smile returned quickly. Why was he so sour? "Good! You saw the empty trunk?" she asked.

"Yes."

"Do you ever say more than yes or no?" she said tauntingly, much to the delight of the giggling children.

Devin's mouth now twisted into a sardonic smile. Why couldn't he take his eyes from hers? Their emerald-green depths seemed to hold him, overpower him. She was a strikingly beautiful woman. And she *was* only five feet tall. Why did he feel this strange heat, as if he had stepped into a fast-boiling caldron? "Sometimes," he answered finally, bringing more laughter from the children.

"Ah," Bonnie said, nodding sagely. At least he was

11

a good sport. She smiled at him. "I see." Opening a small trapdoor in the top of the black trunk, she said, "Please reach inside, Dr. Warner."

"It's empty," he said with confidence before doing as he was asked. He had seen the empty trunk. This wasn't a stage. A solid concrete floor lay under their feet. At most he expected to find some silk scarves inside or some other easily concealed trickery. He put his hand through the trapdoor and felt inside, prepared to go along with the gag for the sake of the children. His eyes widened. He barely suppressed a gasp of surprise.

"Come on, Dr. Warner. Pull something out!" Bonnie prompted, more delighted than usual with the baffled look on her mark's face. He was really *very* attractive.

Scarcely able to believe his own eyes, Devin pulled a stuffed toy rabbit from the trunk. He handed it to Bonnie, who handed it to the nearest child.

"Again, please," she instructed.

Again and again Devin reached into the "empty" trunk to retrieve a stuffed animal, until all the children had one. "Empty?" Bonnie asked, enjoying the look of chagrin on her reluctant assistant's face.

"Yes," he announced with finality.

"Really?" she asked slyly.

"I mean—I . . ." Groping inside the trunk, he came up with a pink carnation, which Bonnie took from him and pinned to his lapel. "Now it's empty," he said, startled at how much he was enjoying the touch of her graceful hands. "I think," he added cautiously.

"Yes." Bonnie looked around at the happy faces of the children playing distractedly with their new toys. "Magic!" she stage-whispered. Amid laughter and applause she pulled her trunk from the room, followed by Devin a few moments later.

Out in the corridor, after some carefully concealed movements, Bonnie handed an orderly her keys and thanked him for taking the trunk out to her car. "No peeking," she reminded him cheerfully as he lugged the trunk down the hall. "Magicians set traps for the overcurious."

Devin watched the proceedings, wondering why he was still standing there. He had work to do. But something made him linger, made him go up and tap this delightfully enchanting woman on the shoulder. Perhaps he just wanted another look at those striking eyes of hers. Eyes, after all, were his business. "Thanks for the flower," he said, uncharacteristically tongue-tied. Standing next to her he had that odd feeling again, as if he were standing near an electrical transformer. He shook the feeling off.

Bonnie turned to him. "You're welcome, Dr. Warner." Amusement played across her features. She had purposely dawdled, hoping he would speak to her again. He had the most alluring voice, even if he did appear cynical.

She didn't look surprised to see him. For some reason her self-assurance annoyed him. "How did you do that, Miss . . ."

"Tyson. Call me Bonnie," she replied, holding out her hand.

They shook hands, each one noticing a certain

resemblance: Both had long, strong fingers. Devin's were more muscular, Bonnie's more classically graceful; but talent, skill, and dexterity were obviously attributes they shared.

Each also noticed a certain reluctance to let the other's hand go. Devin felt somewhat embarrassed by this reluctance; Bonnie obviously didn't. Again he found himself mildly annoyed and wondering why.

Devin's annoyance disappeared when she smiled at him, though—a smile that touched those marvelous eyes. "Tyson." He repeated the name a few times under his breath. "The Mysterious Tyson?" he queried.

"My father," she acknowledged. "He doesn't perform anymore, but his magic and his stage name live on in me." She bowed dramatically, her silk outfit a billowing white cloud. "Are you interested in magic?"

"It's an . . . amusing way to make a living."

Again that sour tone in his voice—was it displeasure? Her pale eyebrows furrowed. "You disapprove?"

Devin pursed his lips. "I just wonder if it's wise to practice your, um, trade in hospital wards," he replied.

Disbelief replaced Bonnie's frown. She thought of all the happy, smiling faces she had just left. "The children were—"

"Excited," he interrupted. "They're here because they're ill. They need rest, not excitement."

Words formed themselves in her mind as her temper came dangerously near the boiling point. *Pompous. Arrogant.* She bit the words back and spoke calmly: "I always clear my shows with the chief of staff, Dr. Warner." Here she was, thinking he had wanted to meet her and sensing a special kind of spark between them. Her instincts were rarely wrong, but obviously they were this time. He was actually chastising her for bringing these children some happiness!

Devin shrugged carelessly. "That's her decision, of course. But I'm not on staff here, so I can speak my mind." He was just offering his opinion. Why was she so upset? He could practically *feel* her anger. "I only said I wondered whether the excitement was good for them."

"All my magic isn't in my trunk, Doctor. I bring light and laughter into their lives. It makes them feel better!" Bonnie asserted, still grappling with her temper.

He nodded impatiently. "I know that's the popular opinion in some circles right now, but it isn't mine. The only thing that helps these children get well is medication, rest, and the care of a qualified physician."

Bonnie stared at him in amazement. Had he just stepped out of a time machine from the past? "How old are you, Dr. Warner?"

"Thirty-eight. Why?"

"That's funny. I would have guessed by your attitude that you were at least one hundred!"

Devin decided it was true what they said about performers. They really were temperamental. "I didn't mean to offend you, Bonnie. I'm only stating my opinion." He wasn't used to apologizing, but he did feel an unusually strong desire to get to know this woman better. And so lovely did she look when she was angry, this confrontation wasn't getting him any closer to see-

15

ing what was behind her mystical facade. He decided to go back to his original question. "Now, about that trunk. How did you do it?"

Bonnie, despite her strong attraction to this opinionated disbeliever, was still furious. She remembered the look of astonishment on his face when he had found all those stuffed animals in her trunk. For all his distrust he was still susceptible to that flicker of doubt, that willingness of even the most inflexible mind to believe the impossible. It was time, she thought, to teach him a lesson. No one messed with a sorcerer! "Magic!" she whispered.

"No, really—" He stopped, startled by the strange gleam in her eyes.

"Yes, really!" She shot her hands straight up, allowing her sleeves to fall to her shoulders and displaying her bare arms. "Nothing up my sleeve," she announced. She held her hands straight out, with fists clenched, and then opened them with the palms up. Sitting in each palm was a small blue sphere. She closed her hands, then opened them again. One palm was empty, the other held the two spheres. Again she closed her hands, and when she opened them, they were both empty.

Devin blinked in surprise, even though he tried very hard not to. With a sigh he looked back to her face. He had spent enough valuable time on this nonsense. "You're very skilled, Bonnie. I'd like to see more. How—"

"You want me to go to lunch with you? That's nice, but I'm afraid I can't." Seeing his eyebrows shoot up, she laughed. "Don't believe in mind reading either, I see."

How had she done that? He *was* about to ask her to lunch. It was that damned self-assurance of hers again, he decided. "Now, Bonnie—"

"Now, Devin," she mimicked.

He looked down at his coat pocket. His name tag said only Dr. Warner, Ophthalmology. He hadn't told her his first name, and no one at the hospital called him anything but Dr. Warner. He fought against a totally new feeling for him—bewilderment. "I was just—"

"You were just hungry and thought I might be too?" she offered blithely. A small group of hospital staff had gathered around them by now. The performer in Bonnie couldn't resist showing off. It was at Devin's expense, but she figured he deserved it. She held her palm out again. This time a small flame burned at its center. "I cooked something up earlier. A magician rarely needs a stove."

The crowd around them gasped. Devin looked concerned. "That's enough. Fun's fun, but that's dangerous," he said sternly, pointing to the flame.

"Is it?" she asked. In a quick movement she put her hand to his cheek.

Devin shied away, but when her palm touched his face it was no warmer than a woman's hand should be. A part of his mind felt her touch, enjoyed it; the rest of him reeled in confusion. Confusion was another feeling he wasn't used to, and he didn't enjoy it at all. "Damn it!"

Permitting herself a small smile of triumph for finally breaking into his self-confident little world, Bonnie moved her hands down the front of his lab coat. "My, you are hungry. Here," she said, producing an apple from nowhere and handing it to him. She leaned close to whisper in his ear: "Magic!"

As she walked away, amid exclamations of amazement and quietly clapping hands, Devin watched her, still feeling the touch of her hand, the warmth of her breath against his ear. When she was gone, he had trouble convincing himself anything had really happened. He felt for the carnation, to prove to himself she had been there at all. It, too, was gone.

CHAPTER TWO

Dr. Devin Warner, Bonnie thought as she climbed into her car. Stuffed shirt. With great relish she recalled the look of astonishment on his face. It hadn't really been mind reading, of course, though there was always a certain feeling she got when she did that sort of thing, an eerie feeling. She was, as her father had often told her, almost too good at it.

From the time she was twelve years old she had performed with her world-famous father, and before that she had spent a great deal of time simply learning at his knee. There were subtle cues in people's voices that spoke volumes to the trained ear, the observant listener. And Bonnie was nothing if not observant. In addition to watching and being intensely aware of everything around her, she also read several newspapers daily, one of which had recently run a story on the pioneering eye surgeon Dr. Devin Warner. She imagined he really hadn't been so much startled by her knowing his first name as annoyed by her using it in front of the hospital staff.

She joined a line of cars waiting to exit the hospital parking lot, still a bit annoyed herself. He didn't believe in magic of any kind, obviously, not even the magic laughter could bring to a sick child. Now, *that* did surprise her, and accounted for her blatantly theatrical display of righteous indignation. She was accustomed to skeptics, thrived on them actually. After all, what fun would it be if everybody were as easily convinced, as ready to believe, as were the children who so often comprised her audiences? But Devin's skepticism ran so deep, encompassed so much. What *does* he believe in? she wondered. Only himself and his own skills, probably. That kind of self-centered philosophy wasn't unheard of in the medical profession.

Bonnie realized there could be other reasons for his curious attitude, which seemed to her a mixture of interest and subtle standoffishness. A lot of people believed that magicians were some kind of charlatan—a held-over memory of traveling medicine shows, she supposed. Such people grouped magicians, jugglers, fortune-tellers, and gypsies into one unsavory category, viewing them with either distrust or superstitious awe. She usually didn't bother about justifying herself to them. So why had she reacted so strongly to this particular skeptic?

"An amusing way to make a living," she muttered to herself as she pulled onto the Interstate heading south out of Denver. As usual, the traffic was horrendous at lunchtime. She decided it wasn't so much what he had said as the way he had said it. There was such . . . such distaste in his voice! She had started to tell him she didn't make her living with magic. She only performed in hospitals or for benefits. Her father had made an "amusing" amount of money with his skill, and she supported her addiction to public works with the substantial trust he had set up for her. But she doubted that telling Devin any of this would have changed his opinion of her. He didn't seem to think much of her visits to the children, anyway. Well, who cared what he thought!

So, if she didn't care what his opinion of her was, why did she continue to think about him? Because, she thought, just because. Along with her unusual ability to practically reach into people's minds, she had another ability—she preferred to think of it as a skill: an uncanny knack for judging character. And somehow something inside told her Dr. Devin Warner wasn't nearly so firm a believer in the well-ordered universe as he would like everyone to think he was. If there was one thing Bonnie couldn't resist it was the challenge of convincing a skeptic, especially one with such a carefully guarded chink in his armor. All that and a sexy devil too, she thought. No wonder she was still thinking about him!

The seventy or so miles from Denver to Colorado Springs passed quickly with such thoughts to occupy her mind. Traveling never bothered her. With her father and mother she had been almost everywhere in the world at least once. She had seen and done more things, met and talked with more people of different cultures, than most individuals twice her thirty years. Still, as always, it was good to get home.

Bonnie had a shop in a renovated Victorian house that held several other small businesses—artists' studios mainly. From this shop she sold coffee, tea, and herbs. She thought of her business as a hobby, really, something to keep her occupied and in touch with the public; and she took pleasure in every aspect of it—the shop, its carefully nurtured atmosphere of exotic mystery—with the childlike abandon of one who didn't need it to make much of a profit. It made a nice one anyway.

At the front door Bonnie paused to enjoy the sunlight streaming through the black lace curtains and inhale the aromatic fragrance of Colombian coffee, fruit-flavored teas, garlic, marjoram, and a thousand other herbs and spices. Her mind's eye saw an open-air market in Rangoon, boat peddlers in Bangkok, the swirl of bright silk in downtown Kowloon.

"That'll be thirty-five cents." The sprightly voice preceded the speaker, a young woman who now passed through the beaded curtain separating the selling area from the back room.

"What?" Bonnie asked, startled back from her mental travels.

"Five cents a sniff."

"No wonder I'm turning a profit, Marcie," Bonnie observed wryly, "with you running the place while I'm gone. I'm surprised you don't charge admission at the door."

"That's next week," Marcie replied. She was a diminutive woman—though she maintained she had a few inches on her employer—with short black hair and sparkling brown eyes. Dressed in forest-green as she was now, she reminded Bonnie of a subdued leprechaun, an image that probably had more to do with her impish nature than with her stature or attire. "I thought I'd let our bizarre patrons get used to the idea first."

"Bizarre? Oh, come now, Marcie. What's so bizarre about grinding your own coffee or buying fresh herbs?" Bonnie asked, setting down her purse and running a total on the cash register.

"Listen, anyone who buys garlic powder by the five-pound bag and doesn't own a restaurant, I'd classify as bizarre."

"Five pounds!" Bonnie laughed. "I suppose I'd call that a bit odd myself. Maybe they have a problem with vampires."

"One thing they won't have a problem with is crowded elevators," Marcie observed.

"No, I suppose not."

Despite Marcie's protests Bonnie closed down the shop and they had lunch in the restaurant on the ground floor. They rounded out their meal with a cookie purchased from Just Cookies, another shop occupying space in the rambling Victorian house. The cookie shop was the first of a large chain owned by Bonnie's friend Amy Tanner. Amy and her husband, Cole, were off on what they would probably later come to appreciate as being a much needed vacation before the arrival of their first child. Bonnie missed Amy's companionship. Perhaps, she thought, she just missed giving the advice Amy seemed constantly in need of.

Bonnie often found herself on the receiving end of other people's stories of woe and worry. They seemed to seek her out, drawn perhaps by her caring nature, or her sophistication, or the aura of mystery that she cultivated. They didn't get their palms read or their tarot cards dealt, but they seldom went away feeling any the worse for having talked to her. It was because of her experience in the ways of the world—and her unfailing optimism—that she had developed the philosophy that seemed to comfort them. "Things have a way of working out for the best," she was fond of saying. "No matter how hard you try to stop them."

After lunch, in-between customers, Marcie played sorcerer's apprentice. Bonnie was slowly teaching her the magical arts. Very slowly. She found her student somewhat lacking in patience.

The coin in Marcie's hand glinted in the light of the afternoon sun. She closed her hand, opened it, and the coin was gone. "There! How's that?"

Bonnie hummed doubtfully. "Not so good."

In frustration Marcie slapped the coin on the counter before her. "Oh, hell! Only you could find fault with my technique."

Bonnie chuckled indulgently between sips from a cup of chamomile tea. "There's always someone in every audience, Marcie dear, who will be watching your every move, no matter how hard or how well you try to misdirect their attention." She smiled soothingly. "Try it again."

Marcie tried it again, and again, several times before Bonnie nodded her approval. Even then, and well after they had closed up shop, Bonnie wasn't concentrating fully on anything that was going on around her. Her mind was on a certain pair of blue eyes, a certain person in the crowd whose eyes would undoubtedly always be on the lookout for trickery.

All the way home she scolded herself for being absurd. After her performance that morning Devin Warner wouldn't come within ten feet of her, even if she should encounter him again, which was doubtful at best. He lived in Denver, and though she made the rounds of the hospitals there from time to time, it was hardly likely that they would ever run into each other again. And even if they did, she thought—annoyed that she had been so impetuous earlier—Devin would probably see her coming and run the other way. Damn! Why hadn't she swallowed her indignation and gone to lunch with him?

The next day Bonnie had the shop to herself. Marcie, who seemed to have an endless variety of interests, was a part-time business student and was working toward an MBA. It never ceased to amaze Bonnie how Marcie could balance so many different philosophies into one rock-steady personality. An avid interest in magic didn't usually accompany a sharp business mind. Bonnie's father, for instance, had been highly successful in the business of performing. But unlike Marcie, he owed his success more to his great talent and a good manager than to business acumen. Perhaps Marcie only wanted to learn magic to baffle any opponents she might encounter on her rise in the corporate world.

Business, as usual, was brisk in the morning, then slacked off around lunch. Bonnie got a hot dog from a street vendor out front, ate it, then went and purchased another. She knew what was in them, but couldn't seem to help herself. In spite of her herb teas and trim figure, she was a dedicated fan of food—all kinds of food. She was at the front counter giving considerable attention to her next bite of the hot dog when a man walked through the front door, conservative suit and all.

"Do you have any Egyptian basil?" Devin asked before realizing whom he was talking to. He blinked. Twice. "Oh, God, it can't be." He groaned in disbelief.

Bonnie, her mouth full of hot dog, was equally amazed. "Mmph!"

"Making a frankfurter disappear, I see," he observed sardonically. "Those aren't good for you, you know."

Swallowing desperately, Bonnie smiled, embarrassedly wiping mustard from her chin. "Hi!" she managed at last. Great, Bonnie dear. What a marvelous conversationalist you are! "I—"

"It is you, isn't it, Miss Mysterious Tyson?" There was an unmistakable edge of sarcasm to his voice.

Before she thought to stop herself or could remember her vow to be nicer to Devin should they meet again, she responded in kind: "Surely you didn't come all the way from Denver for basil."

Devin frowned. "What's the matter? Catch you on a bad day?"

His sarcasm lingered. It didn't surprise her, but it did confuse her. "What?" Another marvelous comeback. Wipe the stupid grin off your face and quit staring at him, you idiot!

"I would have thought that, in your infinite wisdom, you knew I lived in the Springs, not Denver."

"Oh." Gee, she thought. I had to go to college to learn to speak like this. Such wit, such brilliance. Seeing him again sent an undeniable thrill through her,

26

and she liked the feeling. But she had to break free of the spell Devin's blue eyes were working on her. Basil. He wanted basil.

Stepping from behind the counter, Bonnie went to the shelves lining one wall of the shop. Devin watched as she climbed up on a ladder to reach the jar she wanted. She had made a fool of him yesterday, but now he felt his anger fade as that strange sensation of heat flowed through him again. Maybe she really *was* a sorcerer. He certainly felt bewitched.

She was wearing a peasant dress, its black gauzelike fabric decorated with intricate embroidery in brilliant colors. Without thinking—indeed unable to stop himself—Devin put his hands around her slim waist and helped her down from the ladder.

His touch did odd things to her insides. Odd, but very pleasant. "Thank you."

Devin nodded, caught once again in the emerald web of her gaze. But when she stepped toward him, he took a step back, and all bets were off. "What are you doing?" he asked warily.

The upper hand at last! "Just showing you the basil," she replied, clearly amused. She took another step forward.

Devin took another step back. "Not going to light me on fire? Turn me into a toad? Make my ears disappear?"

Bonnie laughed. "Hardly. But I might strangle you with your tie if you don't stop. I got a bit carried away yesterday. I'm sorry."

She had a lovely laugh, he noticed. Full and deep. Sexy. "Are you really?"

27

"No."

"Ha!"

With a swirl of her long skirt Bonnie returned to the counter and set down the jar of basil. She smiled at him innocently. "Feel better with me over here?" she asked.

"Much." Actually, he had felt better with his hands on her full hips. The feelings he had when close to her were rapidly becoming a sort of addiction, and a very nice one.

"You just made me mad, with your . . . opinion of my work at the hospital," she explained. "I *did* over-react." Her smile broadened. "A bit," she amended.

"I was overzealous." Devin returned her smile. "A bit."

They both laughed, realizing that neither had actually apologized. Devin approached the counter with exaggerated caution.

"I've been in before but I've never seen you. Do you work here part-time?" he asked.

"I work here when the mood suits me or when my assistant's schedule demands it. I own the shop," Bonnie explained.

Devin's brow arched in surprise. "I thought—"

"That I was a full-time magician?" she interrupted.

"Here we go again," he returned in a tone of playful disgust. He looked around the shop as if for the first time.

"Now you're going to ask where I keep the bats' wings and eye of newt."

"Aha! Caught you!" he said gleefully. "I was going to ask how you came to open a store like this."

What a paradox the man was, Bonnie thought. He wasn't nearly as stiff and straight as she'd first thought. But the different facets of his character revealed themselves slowly, subtly. "My mother is very knowledgeable about herbs. Her Irish folk heritage, I suppose. She got me interested in them, and the coffee and teas just came along afterward. Now they're the biggest part of my business."

Bonnie studied the tie he was wearing. At first glance she thought it had a subtle pattern of muted green dots. Closer inspection showed each dot to be a tiny frog. Was this yet another telltale sign, this time revealing a possible penchant for the whimsical? "That's quite a tie you have there," she announced, unable to conceal a teasing grin.

"What's the matter?" Devin asked. "Doesn't it go with the suit?"

"It looks fine. It's just that it hardly fits your ultra-conservative image."

Devin looked perturbed for a moment, then smiled. "That's the whole idea, actually. My older patients like the dark suits, but they sometimes scare my younger patients, so I usually wear something a bit crazy to lighten the mood," he explained.

"Sort of an eye test for the children you treat?" Bonnie asked. Devin nodded and laughed, and Bonnie decided she wasn't just attracted to Devin Warner, she liked him too.

Devin ended up buying some coffee, his Egyptian basil, and garlic powder. Bonnie was glad to see he didn't buy it by the five-pound bag. His purchases all neatly wrapped, Devin found himself very reluctant to leave. Here was one very intriguing woman, and he wasn't going to let her mysterious persona deter him. "Are you reading my mind right now?" he asked, gazing at her smiling face with its astonishingly high cheekbones.

"Oh, Devin," she said, exasperated.

"No, really. Do you know what I'm going to ask you?"

She had a pretty good idea but kept quiet and shook her head no.

"Will you have dinner with me this evening?"

"Yes."

"That was quick. Don't you even want to know where?"

"Oh, I eat anything," she said with a chuckle, picking up the remnants of her hot dog. "Just don't put too much of that basil in whatever it is you're cooking for us."

Devin's eyes widened. "How did you know . . ." he began in a startled voice. His eyes narrowed. "You really like to keep people guessing, don't you?"

"So I've been told," she replied, a wicked sparkle in her eyes.

Bonnie pulled her car up in front of Devin's house at seven thirty that evening, filled with delicious anticipation. When he had told her his address earlier, they had both been startled to discover they were almost neighbors. Nestled against the base of the Rocky Mountains, their houses were no more than a mile apart. In fact, Bonnie had driven by Devin's place countless times before, admiring the avant-garde architecture of the geometrically shaped building. When Devin ushered her graciously through the front door, she found that the interior was equally modern but unexpectedly homey and comfortable. She liked it immediately.

"I've always wondered what this house looked like on the inside," she commented when Devin proudly gave her a tour. "It's very unusual."

He chuckled. "Is that good or bad?"

"Good. It's modern without all that cold chrome interior decorators are so fond of these days. I prefer wood."

Devin poured her a glass of white wine and looked admiringly at her hands when she accepted it from him. "I'm glad you like my house," he said, now watching her graceful movements as she wandered around the living room. She was wearing an alluring silk blouse and a skirt of multicolored silk. Her smooth, glossy hair hung loose down her back. When she turned to face him again, her eyes sparkled with life. "When I first saw your eyes, I thought you must wear green contacts," Devin said. "But that's your natural color."

"Twenty-twenty vision," she said, smiling. "Oh," she added, going to the couch where she had left her purse, "I almost forgot." She went over to him again and pinned a pink carnation to his sweater vest. It looked a bit out of place—she had expected the usual conservative suit, not his slacks, shirt, and sweater oufit—but he seemed quite pleased.

"Thank you." He pursed his lips, observing her with quiet humor. "I suppose I'm lucky you don't lead

31

a life of crime. With your touch you'd make an excellent pickpocket."

"How do you know I'm not one?" she asked slyly.

Purely as a reflex, Devin patted his hip for his wallet, found it still in his possession, and laughed. "Let's make a deal for this evening. I won't talk about eye surgery if you won't practice magic on me. Okay?" he asked, smiling broadly.

"Deal."

No matter what she said, Devin thought, she was still working some kind of magic on him. He had never been so wildly attracted to a woman. And something told him the feeling was mutual. "So you do stop performing sometimes?" He led the way to the couch and took a seat.

Bonnie sat beside him, sipping the good white wine. "Of course. Does that surprise you?"

"You do have a—this sounds so trite," he muttered. "A kind of mysterious air about you even now," he finished, enjoying her smile.

"I know."

Devin looked startled. "You mean you work at it?"

"Not work at it exactly. It's more second nature to me," she explained amiably. "Rather like *your* air of unquestionable authority."

"Touché."

"You have to take my background into account."

"Oh?" He was all ears, wanting to know anything, everything, about her.

She arched her brow dramatically. "My father is a conjurer, my mother a white witch. I was born in Tibet on a snowy mountaintop with a full moon overhead. How's that for a childhood environment?"

Devin chuckled at her flippant attitude. "Tibet? Really?"

"Really. My parents were there studying the myths and legends of the area. All the hiking they did brought my mother into labor sooner than expected."

"It's odd," Devin said, looking at her curiously, "but for all your mystical persona, I think I detect a bit of skepticism in your voice."

"Oh, I am a skeptic," Bonnie agreed. "There's nothing like traveling all over the world with a pair like my parents to give you a good, healthy sense of disbelief. It's one thing to watch magic, another to perform it. But," she added in a warning tone, her eyes taking on that strange gleam again, "I've also seen and experienced things that would stand your hair on end. I'm skeptical, not cynical."

"Implying that I am, I suppose?"

" 'There are more things in heaven and earth, Horatio, than are dreamt of in your philosophy.' "

"Uh-huh," Devin replied noncommittally.

Bonnie laughed. "As for you, my practicing cynic, I think there may be more of a belief in the impossible in you than you care to let on."

Devin loved her laugh, but he wished she would change the subject. "Oh, I'm not practicing, I'm a professional," he asserted. "Comes with the degree. In medicine you have to investigate, probe, study. You believe only what your senses and experience tell you, and often only half of that."

Bonnie frowned. "What about instinct, intuition,

those flashes of insight they say lead to medical break-throughs?"

Devin waved her question aside. "That's just a lay-man's explanation for a subconscious thought process. The years of training don't all stay on the surface. Some knowledge becomes submerged but is later brought to life by certain situations, unanswered questions, or astute observation. It just depends on who's doing the observing, a superstitious primitive or a scientist."

Devin was obviously enjoying this new turn in the discussion. Bonnie wasn't sure if she was or not. She had the vague feeling that she had just been insulted. She decided, however, that it was true about opposites attracting. Devin and she were certainly opposites, and they were certainly attracted to each other. The big question in her mind at the moment was how well they would be able to get along when their philosophies of life were so different. She wanted to get along with him, but his narrow-minded views would make it difficult. "And how would you account for the unexplained?" she said, returning to the conversation.

"The unexplained is just that," he answered confidently. "Something for which there is no explanation. Yet. We use magnets for everything from electric motors to holding notes on refrigerators, but magnetic attraction itself is still something of a mystery. That doesn't prevent us from using the phenomenon to our advantage in a calm, rational manner," he finished, obviously pleased with his analogy.

Bonnie wondered how he would explain the almost magnetic attraction they had for each other. She decided she didn't want to hear the feelings she had right now explained in scientific terms. "So it's mysterious but not mystical, right?"

"Right."

She grinned, then turned the tables on him. "And that bothers you, doesn't it? The fact that something so simple could remain so mysterious."

"Bothers me? Yes, I suppose—I—" he sputtered.

"Come on, Devin, admit it," she urged playfully. "Your philosophy of the little mysteries of life may be logical, but it doesn't comfort you at all, now, does it?"

"Well—"

"Does it?" she taunted, seeing by his expression that she had scored a point.

Devin sighed with frustration. "Dinner should be ready. I'll go take a look."

"Ha!" she exclaimed triumphantly. Magician one, scientist zero.

"And for your information," Devin said haughtily as he made his way to the kitchen, "you're not as good a mind reader as you think. You decided I was cooking dinner tonight because I bought basil from you this afternoon."

"But I was right! You are cooking dinner."

"Only half right. One doesn't put *any* basil into coq au vin." Actually, he usually did but had left it out this time to spite her.

Bonnie was in for still another surprise: Devin turned out to be a wonderful cook. More than that, he enjoyed puttering around in the kitchen. As they talked over dinner, carefully avoiding any more philo-

35

sophical discussions, she found that her sense of liking him, apart from his attraction, was growing. He was fairly well traveled himself, had a dry sense of humor she appreciated, and wasn't as consumed by his profession as she had first thought. All in all, it was a very enjoyable and enlightening meal.

"More wine?" Devin offered when they returned to the living-room sofa.

"No, thank you. I'm performing tomorrow," Bonnie replied.

He chuckled. "And I'm operating. How about coffee?"

"I'd prefer herb tea if you have any."

"Just one of those boxed brands with the soothing names," he said uncertainly, remembering her shop and the rows and rows of teas. "Is that okay?"

"Sure. Remind me to give you some of my special mix the next time you visit the shop," she said as she followed him to the kitchen.

"Witches' brew?" he joked.

"Something like that. Need any help?" She watched him from the doorway, liking what she saw. Devin wasn't what she would call stocky, but he was quite strongly built for a man so involved in intellectual pursuits. He had probably been very athletic when he was in school, and obviously still was. She found herself wondering if the rest of him was as tanned and well muscled as the forearms revealed by his rolled-up shirt sleeves. She also found that she had an incredibly strong urge to find out.

Devin seemed uncomfortable about having anyone

in his kitchen. "I'll manage," he replied to her offer of help.

She saw now that she would only have been in the way. He had a very methodical way of doing things—everything in its place and a place for everything. She went back to the couch where he joined her shortly with a tray set with a teapot, cups, and a pot of honey.

For a few moments they sipped their tea in a surprisingly companionable silence for two people who had only met—and rather brusquely—the day before. It was rare to be so comfortable with a relative stranger, and Bonnie knew it. She enjoyed the feeling.

"So"—Devin spoke at last—"you've been a professional traveling magician for most of your life?"

"All through my teens when school permitted, then pretty much full-time after college. I was my father's apprentice, and before that I worked as his assistant alongside my mother."

"That's something of a time-honored position among magicians, isn't it? Sorcerer's apprentice, I mean."

Bonnie chuckled at his choice of words. "Yes. My father began serving his apprenticeship at the tender age of eight."

"You have a rather precocious skill yourself," he noted wryly, thinking of her dramatic flair at the hospital.

"I have a knack for it," she explained as she poured herself and Devin another cup of tea. "Not to mention loads of practice. The Mysterious Tyson's stage productions were quite complicated and dramatic. Performing requires a great deal of hard work."

37

Devin added more honey to his tea. "Is that why your father retired?"

"It's a demanding profession, one that had been his life for over forty years. Gradually I took over the act as he made his graceful exit. I was on my own by the time I was twenty-six."

He laughed. "You must have been very precocious indeed! How old is your father now?"

"Sixty. He's still a very dramatic and energetic man. My mother and he spend most of their time pursuing their mutual passion, the myths and legends of ancient civilizations."

Devin cleared his throat. "Does he, um, approve of the direction you've taken since his retirement?"

Bonnie knew what was making him uneasy. "You mean the hospital visits. He thinks it's wonderful," she replied. A flash of defiance awoke in her eyes.

Sitting so close to this beautiful, enigmatic woman, her exotic scent tempting him with every move she made, Devin decided that the last thing he wanted then was to antagonize her. "Where are you performing tomorrow?" he asked, hoping to change the subject.

Bonnie wondered how he would react if she told him, another children's hospital. Luckily, she didn't have to confront that issue yet. "I'm doing a benefit for the Special Olympics. A sort of fund-raiser down at the City Auditorium."

He looked approving but surprised. "You still do full stage shows too?"

"More often than I'd like, really. I enjoy smaller audiences, the close-up magic. Stage shows are such big productions, and you can't identify with the audience as well, or get them to identify with you. But," she said with a sigh, "they do bring in the money, so I continue doing them." She grinned at him impishly. "Where are you performing tomorrow?"

Devin looked startled, then he laughed with her. "I suppose you could call an operation a performance of sorts. They don't call surgery the operating theater much anymore, but that's what it seems like sometimes. You have your assistants, your props, and in teaching hospitals you even have an audience." He looked at her with a warm smile. "I even get something akin to stage fright on occasion."

"You?" She could picture him angry, perturbed, and she'd certainly seen him baffled, but if Devin didn't present the very image of the fearless surgeon, no one did. Except, she thought with some satisfaction, when it came to being a bit leery of her magic.

"Sometimes. I use it to my advantage, though. I find it gives me an edge—sharpens my senses."

Imagine Devin using an intangible element like nervousness to help him in his work! "I know what you mean. A little stage fright sharpens my wits too. No matter how many times I do an illusion, there's always the chance that—"

"The trick won't work?" he interrupted.

"That the *magic* won't work," she corrected slyly.

Devin threw back his head and laughed. Bonnie decided he should let himself go more often; somehow it made him even more attractive. "You really are something else, Miss Mysterious Tyson," he informed her, still chuckling. "Every time I think I have you pinned down, you slip away."

Bonnie didn't slip away when he moved closer to her, though. She was enjoying the warmth of his thigh against hers, the heat of his gaze.

He took her hand in his. "You have the most beautiful eyes," he said softly.

"Yours are pretty nice too," she returned, unexplainably shy. She lost her shyness when his head dipped and his lips brushed hers lightly. She tried vainly to make her pulse slow down, then gave in, parting her lips to Devin's delicately probing tongue. It wasn't much of a surrender; she had been waiting to taste his kiss all evening.

Despite her pliant response, Devin pulled back. "I'm sorry."

"Sorry?" she murmured dreamily, allowing her hands to wander to the back of his neck.

"I didn't mean to pounce on you like that," he said, wondering what had come over him, but unable to ignore the delicious feel of her graceful fingers on the nape of his neck.

Wrapping her arms around him, urging him closer, she replied in a husky voice, "Don't stop."

He didn't take much convincing. Embracing her, turning her willing form to press her closely against his chest, he kissed her again, deeper, his tongue lingering, drinking in her sweetness. Through the thin silk of her blouse she felt his hand running the length of her spine—a sensation so pure she might have been wearing nothing at all. Feeling the taut muscles of his back through the unyielding barrier of his clothing,

40

she could get no more than a tantalizing taste of what it would be like to caress his bare skin. The strength of her desire startled Bonnie, indeed gave her pause.

"Now *I'm* sorry for pouncing on you," she said breathlessly when their lips parted at last.

"Really?" he asked, obviously finding it just as difficult to catch his breath.

"No."

"Ha!" It was a soft exclamation, its tone more sensual than triumphant.

Bonnie's hands wandered down his chest, once again finding her explorations frustrated. The thickness of his vest got in the way of her sensitive, probing fingers. She wanted more. "So," she said slyly, "when do you operate tomorrow?"

"I wish you hadn't said that," he answered with frustration and dismay. "I have to be on the far side of Denver by six tomorrow morning, and I have about an hour's worth of work to finish a lecture I'm giving tomorrow afternoon."

Seeing the look of distress on his face, Bonnie herself wished she hadn't said anything. Giving herself a mental kick in the pants, she quickly calculated the time: a two-hour drive, an hour's worth of work, and it was now ten o'clock. He would barely get five hours' sleep, even if he was one of those infuriating people who could drop off quickly. "It's late. I'd better—"

"No." Devin pulled her back into his arms, his voice soft and persuasive. "I don't need much sleep. Stay for a while."

If she stayed she knew neither of them would get any sleep at all. It didn't take much imagination to see

41

where strong mutual attraction was leading them. "Oh, no you don't," she asserted, managing to free herself from his tempting grasp. "I'm not going to be the cause of a sleepy surgeon."

"I can handle it. Really. Doctors get accustomed to no sleep early on in med school." He rose with her and pulled her into his arms again, planting a sweet trail of kisses along her throat.

Bonnie shivered with delight, but her resolve held firm, though she didn't know how. "Absolutely not. Besides, I have a stage show tomorrow. I have so much to do I'll probably be up and running before you even hit the highway." It was true, she supposed, or largely true. Damn it!

Slowly, reluctantly, and in very obvious frustration, Devin let her go. "I suppose you're right. For such a well-organized person, I have rotten timing."

They both laughed gratefully, breaking a sexual tension so strong Bonnie felt she could cut it with a knife. "Now that you know I'm not going to make your ears disappear, and I know that you're human, I'm sure we can work on our timing." She picked up her purse and followed him to the door. "In a hurry to get rid of me now, I see," she teased.

"As a matter of fact, I am. I'm all too human, which you'll quickly find out unless you leave. Now!"

They kissed, a long lingering kiss filled with the promise of things to come, then Bonnie took her leave. She tingled all the way home and ended up not sleeping very well anyway. A not entirely unpleasant ache reminded her that she was all too human herself.

CHAPTER THREE

Bonnie rose early the next morning and practiced until it was time to leave for her show that afternoon. The three days that followed were nearly identical, with two shows a day, one in the afternoon and one in the evening. The benefit was a success. Delighted audiences packed the City Auditorium for the worthy cause, and Bonnie was very pleased. She was also happy when Sunday, the last day of the benefit, finally came. There would be no show that night.

Each evening Devin had called, but always from out of town. Finding a way to spend time with each other was somehow beyond them, but their conversations did enable them to get to know each other much better. They spent long evenings on the phone talking about anything and everything.

Sunday night Devin's call seemed to come a bit later than usual, but only because, with no show to do, Bonnie had been waiting anxiously to hear his voice. It was a local call, and he sounded as tired as she felt. But a tickle of excitement ran along her spine when he spoke, for she knew he was now only a mile away.

"It's shattering to realize I don't have the stamina of a med student anymore," he told her sleepily.

"I know how you feel," Bonnie commiserated. "I used to do three shows a night with my father and then party till dawn. In a way, though, I'm kind of glad those days are over."

"Umm. My days as an intern were exciting, but I wouldn't live them over again either. I guess we're both enjoying our old age."

Bonnie chuckled. "Oh, yes. Warm milk and shuffle-board. We're just feeling sorry for ourselves."

"I know I am. I'd like to see you."

"I'd fall asleep in your arms."

"How flattering. Sounds very inviting, though."

Yes, Bonnie thought, it does. "Inviting it might be, but not possible. After the last show this afternoon I mixed with the audience for a while, then I had some work to do at the shop. It's been a very hectic end to a hectic week, and I'm exhausted."

"So am I. I've been either in a car or on my feet since three this morning. Neither of us would make very scintillating company," Devin replied, not believing it for a minute.

Bonnie imagined that somehow, once they were together, they would find energy they didn't know they had. "How about lunch tomorrow? Marcie's got the shop all day."

"Great! You'll have to come by the clinic, though. I'm not sure when my last appointment before noon will end."

"Clinic?" Of course, she thought. She remembered something about a clinic he operated with three or

44

four other doctors. She didn't know why, but she had thought of him as more a teaching doctor, with his frequent traveling, than a day-to-day practitioner.

The next day, shortly before noon, Bonnie found herself looking for his South Side clinic. It wasn't that his directions were faulty, it was just that the clinic turned out to be in an area she still thought of as an open field. She had known about the buildings that had sprung up there in the past few years, but observant as she was, in her mind the business park was still rolling meadow.

Colorado Springs had grown rapidly in the time Bonnie had called the once-small town home. She tended to drive by the rapid-growth areas with only a part of her mind registering the heavy equipment grading the soil, the beginnings of foundations and framework, the final landscaping and parking lots. Then one day she looked at the area and said to herself, How did that get there? She wasn't alone in her surprise. Most of the residents viewed the sprawling growth with varying degrees of either elation or despair. Bonnie viewed it with calm acceptance.

Finding the clinic at last, Bonnie parked her car and went inside, approaching the receptionist. "Excuse me?"

A young blond in a white nurse's uniform looked up. "Name?"

"Bonnie Tyson," she answered without thinking. "But I'm—"

The woman ran her finger down a column of names. "Tyson. Here we are. You're late," she said sorrowfully, noting that it was after twelve.

"I had some trouble finding the place." What was she doing? It was efficient of Devin to inform his staff she would be coming, but hadn't he told them she was only here for a lunch date, not an appointment? "You don't understand, I—"

"Take this and fill it out," the blonde said, handing her a small card and a pen. "Dr. Warner will be with you as soon as he can." She sounded somewhat put out that Bonnie, a new patient, had managed to get an appointment with the busiest doctor in the clinic and hadn't arrived on time.

"But—"

"I'll want the pen back too," she warned before turning her back to Bonnie and disappearing.

"I'll want the pen back too," Bonnie mimicked in an unflattering voice. She took a seat in the waiting room and, with a sigh of resignation, proceeded to fill out the card. At least it was something to do while she waited, though there were some interesting magazines. Why was it that the waiting rooms of eye doctors always had the best reading material, even though most of their patients had problems with their vision?

She had just become engrossed in an article in a recent issue of *Working Woman* when the nurse came to take her card, carefully retrieving her pen as well.

"You didn't put down that you wear contacts," she said, looking at the card.

"I don't," Bonnie answered, not liking her snippy attitude.

"No room for vanity here, um, Bonnie. Tilt your head back."

If she was trying to ingratiate herself with Bonnie

46

by using her first name, the ploy failed miserably. Thinking she wanted proof that her eye color was her own, Bonnie did as asked. "See?"

"Hmm. So you don't." She sounded envious.

Before Bonnie knew what was happening the nurse put drops in her eyes and stuffed a tissue in her hand. "What was that!" she demanded, blinking rapidly and dabbing at her overflowing eyes.

"Dr. Warner wanted your eyes dilated," she answered perfunctorily before pulling her disappearing act again.

Moments later, feeling like a mole that had had its picture taken with a flashbulb, Bonnie was led to a darkened cubicle, muttering epithets about Devin every step of the way. Half sitting, half lying in an oddly designed chair, she plotted dire revenge.

"Hi!" Devin said cheerily, taking a seat on a short stool in front of her.

"Hi yourself," she returned miserably. "As soon as I can see, I'm going to make your ears, nose, and teeth disappear, and not by magic!"

"It's not that bad," Devin assured her soothingly. "How long since you've had your eyes examined?"

"It's on the damn card!" she shot back irritably.

"Hmm. So it is," he replied, clicking his tongue. "Just as I thought. Too long. You people with perfect vision are all alike." Producing a hand-held instrument that looked like a lighted magnifying glass, he came closer. "Let's take a look."

His chair had wheels, and he moved around her, peering into her eyes, periodically telling her to look at different points in the room. He gave her some more drops, positioned a bizarre-looking device in front of her, and moved her up until she was sitting with her chin resting on it. She felt a strange sensation.

"Now what?" she demanded.

"Checking your pressure. You're fine. A very healthy, and gorgeous, pair of eyes." He kissed the tip of her nose.

"Is that part of the examination?" she asked, still miffed.

"Nope. Therapy."

"It didn't help much. I'm still mad at you."

"Therapy for me, not you. I'll take you to lunch wherever you want, to make up for surprising you like this."

"It'll be expensive," she returned vindictively. "And you'll have to read the menu to me."

"You'll be back to normal soon," he assured her.

"Come closer," Bonnie requested. He did so, and she bit him gently on the nose. To her startled enjoyment, he kissed her soundly. She *was* starting to feel better.

After finding out that she still had twenty-twenty vision, they went to lunch. Bonnie's eyesight had cleared nicely, and she was glad. She wouldn't have wanted to miss a single nuance of the envy on the blond nurse's face as Devin and she walked out the door arm in arm.

The restaurant she chose was expensive, even for lunch, but Devin didn't bat an eye. He was too busy gazing at her, marveling at her healthy beauty. Her hair today was French braided, a cornucopia of intricate charm. She had a magnificent color sense, fitting

48

her clothes to her mood seemingly without effort. This afternoon she looked cool and lively in a deceptively simple bone-white sheath of pure silk. Even in pale shades she managed to look mysterious.

"I don't like your nurse," she informed him over dessert.

"I don't think she's awfully fond of you either," he replied, laughing. "Mary's gruff but efficient. And my partners and I aren't exactly the easiest people in the world to work with."

"I suppose it's not an easy job," Bonnie said, feeling a small twinge of compassion. "Even for the short time I was there, I didn't find it a very thrilling place. Some of the people waiting looked pretty apprehensive."

"It's not all bad. Great advances have been made in ophthalmology in the last decade. And for every patient worrying about cataracts or glaucoma, there's one delighted to find they don't need glasses. For that matter, I had a girl in this morning being fitted for contacts. She was very happy."

"Happy?"

"If you need corrective lenses, you need them. And you certainly aren't alone in the world. She was happy because she was getting rid of her clunky old glasses."

"I'm glad my eyes are so healthy," she replied.

"You should be. Eyesight is the sense most often taken for granted. And neglected," he added.

She didn't miss his tone of disapproval. "If you want to see more of me, you don't have to shanghai me into your dark little dungeon. Just call," she replied flippantly.

"I'd like to see more of you, all right," Devin said. The wicked, sensual light in his eyes made Bonnie feel warm all over. He took her hand, his thumb stroking her palm. "A lot more."

Bonnie had never felt such a strong desire to pursue a man, to use all her wiles to make him hers. To tell the truth, she was a little frightened at the strength of her desires. Was she falling in love? She couldn't honestly say she would even know if she was or not. To her, love was real magic, an elusive feeling she had had all too little time to consider in her busy life. One thing she *was* certain of: She liked being with Devin, liked talking to him even when they disagreed, liked touching, and being touched by, him. For now that was reason enough for her to want to know more, feel more. "I'm free the rest of the day," she found herself saying, a hint of smoky sensuality in a voice she barely recognized as her own.

For a moment Devin's eyes locked with hers, communicating a shared desire. Then he sighed—a decidedly masculine sigh of exasperated desperation. "Damn," he muttered under his breath. What was it about her that made him want to chuck all his duties and carry her off to some private world—one with no responsibilities, no patients or phones, no demands on his time. "I see we both have a talent for picking the worst times to get amorous." He spoke with wry amusement. "I have to work. I have appointments this afternoon until six."

"Oh." The disappointment in her voice was plain, but she smiled reassuringly. "Oh, well. Maybe—"

"How about dinner?" Devin interjected hopefully.

Bonnie's tentative smile became a grin. "Now who's the mind reader?"

"No stage shows tomorrow? Command performances for the queen?"

She shook her head. "And you?"

They looked at each other in astonishment as he shook his head no. "You mean we may actually get to spend a whole evening together?" Devin asked doubtfully.

"One can hope," she answered, thrilled by the way he had said "a whole evening."

"Where shall we go?"

That wasn't what Bonnie had in mind at all. "Why don't I cook for you this time?"

"Can you cook?" He looked dubious.

Bonnie's eyes widened mischievously. "You'd look pretty silly without your ears," she warned.

After Devin had gone back to work, Bonnie went shopping. She was determined to show him just how well she could cook, and so she spent the rest of the afternoon preparing for the dinner. They would start with oysters Rockefeller, followed by a salad of crisp mixed greens with a complex herb dressing—an old recipe of her mother's. The main course would be bacon-wrapped filets mignons and homemade bread. Remembering from one of their phone conversations that Devin was enormously fond of chocolate, she decided on a dessert of individual *pots de crème*—thick and rich—and the finest coffee her shop had to offer. And after dinner . . .

Well, she thought, after dinner things would take their natural course. The meal would be rich and filling, but not *too* filling. The oysters, she hoped, would give Devin some ideas of his own about the natural course of things. She herself didn't believe in the oyster's purported qualities as an aphrodisiac, but serving them to him was another kind of magic entirely. Anticipation was the best aphrodisiac!

Cooking for two was much more fun than cooking just for herself, especially when the second person was Devin, but it was still time-consuming. At last Bonnie hung up her apron and took stock of the situation. The salad was chilling in the refrigerator along with the dessert, and on the shelf below, the oysters and meat sat prepared and ready for broiling. The scent of freshly baked bread cooling on the kitchen counter was altogether pleasant and homey. Satisfied, she set the table. Candlelight would create the romantic atmosphere she wanted. Then she went to take a relaxing bubble bath.

While she dressed, Bonnie took a candid look at herself. She wasn't a busty woman, and in a way she had always been thankful for that: a larger bust would be disproportionate to her height. She did have full hips, though, and she took every advantage of her mature curves. Her hair, she knew, was her most dynamic asset, and that evening she let it flow free, almost but not quite concealing the low-scooped back of her pale green dress. The outfit had a dramatically high neckline in front, so the overall effect was at once elegant and daring.

Devin had said he would call when he was finished with his last appointment, so she checked everything twice and sat down to read, trying not to fidget. At half past six she was fidgeting anyway. At seven, when the phone rang, she jumped up expectantly and was more nasty than usual to the salesman at the other end of the line. At seven thirty she was pacing and muttering, her hand on the phone to call Devin when it rang.

"I've, um, hit a couple of snags," he said contritely.

"Don't say it." She felt as if the entire world were conspiring to keep them apart.

"Don't worry, I'll be there," he returned, his voice full of promise. "I was just about to leave, but my car wouldn't start. I had to have it towed in. While I was waiting for the tow truck, I got a—a last-minute appointment," he explained. There was some talking in the background, then Devin spoke again: "I'll be there shortly."

With her luck, he wouldn't be able to get a ride—or worse. Visions of his nurse kidnapping him flashed through Bonnie's mind. "I'll come pick you up."

"I've—" he started, then heard her hang up. "—already got a ride," he finished belatedly.

Bonnie's trip to the clinic was faster this time. Much faster. There was some sort of party next door, however, so she ended up parking a few buildings down from the clinic and walking back. It allowed her to get an unobserved—and unwanted—eyeful of what was going on at the clinic entrance. She halted in her steps, not comprehending what she was seeing.

A willowy brunette was hugging Devin fiercely, and he certainly wasn't objecting. Her shoulder-length hair was blunt cut, and Devin was running his hand over it in a soothing gesture. Bonnie was just able to hear him say, "You're not doing yourself any good, Megan."

53

"I have to keep trying. I have to!" the brunette objected.

Devin released her. He looked angry, but in an oddly gentle way. "We'll discuss it tomorrow."

A door opened in the building next door, so the voices of happy party guests blocked out the rest of the exchange. As Bonnie watched the brunette kiss Devin on the cheek and then head toward the parking lot, she felt an unreasoning anger build within her. Jealousy wasn't an emotion Bonnie had felt often in her life—but then, she had never felt this strongly about a man before. She didn't like the anger inside her, didn't know how to deal with it. Without stopping to apply reason to her actions, she went to confront the brunette.

She was young, perhaps twenty, with a fragile beauty and an open quality about her that disarmed a now very confused Bonnie, who realized she had jumped to conclusions, something she never did. But it was too late to stop now: her purposeful approach had already been noticed. "Excuse me?" Bonnie said hesitantly.

The girl faced her, wide-eyed. "Yes?"

Her eyes were blue, Bonnie noticed, aware, too, of an inexplicable familiarity. "I'm sorry, I didn't mean to startle you," she began, her initial attack now softened into contrite apology. "I just . . ." Her voice trailed off as she studied the brunette's face. "Have we met?" she asked suddenly. What was she doing? She was supposed to be confronting a woman who had just kissed her man! *Her* man? Bonnie fought an unaccustomed blush brought on by her wildly possessive thoughts.

"That's funny, I was just thinking the same thing." The girl cocked her head curiously, then recognition dawned. "The Mysterious Tyson! I saw your show at the Auditorium." There was definite excitement in her young voice. "You were wonderful!"

There were precious few professional female magicians. Bonnie was used to being recognized. But what caused her own, mysterious feeling of recognition? Could she have seen her in the audience? "Thank you."

The young woman extended her hand. "It's an honor to meet you, Ms. Tyson." Seeing the bewildered look on Bonnie's face as they shook hands, she continued: "I'm sorry. My name's Megan. Megan Warner."

It took a good deal of effort on Bonnie's part to keep her mouth from dropping open. At the same time she felt a rush of immense relief as she looked at the girl's facial features and those blue eyes. Devin hadn't mentioned a sister—in fact, had said very little about his family. Then again, she hadn't asked. "Call me Bonnie," she said.

"Bonnie?" Megan repeated in surprise. "When he said he had a date with Bonnie Tyson, I didn't make the connection. Oh!" She began to laugh openly. "Oh, I see. Now I know why you had murder in your eyes when you first came up to me. You must have seen . . ." Her voice trailed off into laughter again.

Embarrassed, Bonnie still found Megan's laughter infectious. "I'm sorry. Devin didn't tell me he had a sister."

55

Megan looked startled. "Oh, please tell him you thought that! Sometimes I think having a daughter my age makes him feel ancient."

There was nothing Bonnie could do to keep her mouth from dropping open this time. Daughter! And, too, it was all she could do to keep from sitting down on the curb in confusion.

Megan glanced at her wristwatch. Bonnie noticed incongruously that she had inherited Devin's long, graceful fingers. "I've got to run. Besides, Dad's been pacing like a caged tiger in there for the last thirty minutes as it is!" she said, her eyes sparkling impishly. "We'll have to get together sometime soon and talk. Imagine! My father dating the Mysterious Tyson."

"But—"

"Bye!" Megan called, already heading for her car. "Have Dad give you my phone number. I've got a lot of questions."

And *she* herself had a lot of questions! Why hadn't Devin told her? With chin determinedly set Bonnie went to find out but stopped short at the door. Their long and increasingly intimate conversations aside, Devin and she were really just getting to know each other. She doubted that he had kept Megan a secret because he was afraid of seeming old, but he must have some reason. She knew he was only thirty-eight. Megan couldn't be more than nineteen or twenty, which would make Devin about eighteen when he fathered her. But there were certainly no signs of a wife now. Although all sorts of wild thoughts were careening through her head, she did feel certain that Devin would have told her if he was married—she was still quite confident of her ability to judge character that far at least. Whatever the situation, it was probably difficult for him to talk about. Should she push it before he was ready to tell her?

It would be better to drop it into the conversation, she decided, her eyes gleaming mischievously: "Oh, by the way, Devin, I met your daughter the other night." Yes. That would be something to see. With a smile, and forcing herself not to think too much about what had just happened, she now walked into the clinic.

Thinking at all became difficult immediately. Whenever she saw Devin she felt an almost overwhelming excitement, and it was doubled now at the thought of spending a romantic evening with him. "Hi!" Really, she thought, I must stop being so talkative.

"I thought something had happened to you," Devin said softly when he turned and saw her.

Something had, she silently agreed, and something was: She was tingling from head to toe. "I—I had trouble getting my car started too. Must be something in the air."

He crossed the waiting room, his long legs taking several swift strides, and grasped her hands in his, holding her at arm's length. "You look wonderful." His eyes roved over her appreciatively. "I'm sorry about all the delay." Reluctantly he released her, then removed his lab coat and shrugged into his suit jacket. "Hungry?"

"Starving."

The look that passed between them communicated what was really on their minds: Both were thinking about something other than food.

"Do you want me to drive?" he asked as he led her out the front door, then paused to lock it and set the burglar alarm.

"What? Oh, no. I'll drive."

Bonnie thought that, having just seen Megan, Devin might be moved to tell her about his daughter, but he didn't mention her. Instead he relaxed in the seat beside her and enjoyed the ride.

"Rough day?" she asked as a way of getting him talking.

"No. Just full of interruptions."

"Like lunch with me?" That was silly. Why had she said that? Now he would think she wanted her ego stroked. Well, she thought, a little stroke about now wouldn't be so bad. Tell me about Megan, damn it!

"Actually," he said, turning her face to his when they stopped for a red light, "my work interfered with our lunch." He kissed her, the pleasant warmth of his lips all too briefly felt as the stoplight turned green.

The warm feeling flooding through her was enough to get them to her house without further questioning. Once there, however, Devin's mind became occupied with other matters.

"What an . . . unusual house," he stated quietly, looking at the rough-cut red stone exterior. "Like a miniature castle."

"I'll take that as a compliment." Her home did look something like a castle, she supposed, with its corner turrets and balconies with stone balustrades. "Come inside," she invited, waving him toward the front door.

"Is it safe?" he asked, seeing the wicked light in those emerald eyes.

"No," she replied saucily. "Not for you."

Devin wrapped his arm around her waist, squeezing her tightly. "I'll risk it anyway."

Bonnie opened the door, her face bathed in the flickering light of a kerosene lamp in the entry hall. "Abandon hope, all ye who enter here."

Devin's eyes took on a dramatic light of their own. "Remind me to tell you about a fantasy I've been having."

"Tell me!"

"Later. Right now you must ply me with food and drink."

They were both ravenous. Devin didn't miss the implication of the first course—the oysters—nor did he fail to remark upon the unusual dressing for the salad. "I have this peculiar feeling you put something in my salad," he said with suspicion, eating every bite anyway.

Bonnie laughed wickedly. "My mother told me that's what my father said when he first tasted the recipe. I was born nine months later." She laughed again at the expression of shock on his face.

By dessert they were both gazing relentlessly into each other's eyes, the rich chocolate and deeply flavored coffee all but forgotten. The candles on the table illuminated their faces and cast shadows on the antique furniture surrounding them in the formal dining room. Devin felt as if he had been magically transported to another place, another time.

"Are you casting a spell on me?" he murmured softly.

"I'm trying," Bonnie replied. She had never been what anyone would call a shrinking violet, but tonight her boldness surprised even her. "Are you in my power?" she asked huskily.

"I am," he replied with an understanding of fate he had never before known himself capable of. They had met by chance at the hospital where he had just stopped by to consult on the patient of a colleague. An hour later and he wouldn't even have been there. It disturbed him greatly to think that he might never have met Bonnie at all, and yet it almost seemed that they were destined to meet. "I am indeed in your power."

"Would you like a tour?"

"Hmm?" He only just managed to pull himself from the drowning depths of her eyes. "Tour?"

"Of the house." Bonnie felt powerful and at the same time weak. She had to order her knees not to buckle when she stood up and took his hand. When he pulled her tight against his chest, a pulse in her throat leapt in response.

"If we must." Devin groaned before pressing his lips to hers, feeling an uncontrolled passion taking hold of his senses. The rational, scientific part of his mind cautioned him. After all, he hadn't known Bonnie all that long. Parts of her personality and her profession still bothered him, worried him. But she was so warm and willing in his arms, her lips as demanding as his own. Strangely, he felt as if he had known her forever, as if he had waited all his life for her. The rational part of his mind wasn't talking loudly enough for him to hear, this evening. His desires and emotions were totally in control.

Bonnie delighted in the feel of his warm, strong hands as they accepted the invitation of the low-scooped back of her dress, caressing her bare skin from the back of her neck to the base of her spine. He might not believe in magic, but he certainly had magic hands, their touch causing her to shiver involuntarily as she arched her body against him.

"I think we'd better take that tour now," she murmured breathlessly against his lips. "I wouldn't want you to get lost." She had envisioned some quiet talk, but now she was dangerously close to speechlessness. The only thing that prevented her from abandoning all thoughts of further conversation was the incident earlier, with Megan. She wanted to know more about this part of his life, and the closer she got to being drawn into this maelstrom of passion, the more she felt she *had* to know.

"I'm already lost," he whispered hoarsely. "I was lost the first time I looked into your eyes." But suddenly Devin felt a certain resistance in her, a resistance that hadn't been there a moment ago. If he believed in such things, he would have sworn Bonnie was sending him a definite mental signal to slow down, even though her soft and pliant body remained excitingly pressed against his. Without fully comprehending why he was doing so, he reluctantly released her. The honest smile on her face as she looked at him reassured him that nothing was wrong. She did look slightly puzzled, though.

"A penny for your thoughts," he said softly.

"A penny?"

"Some of us have to pay to see into other minds," he taunted playfully.

"Mmm." She shook her head. What would he think if she really did tell him what she was thinking—all of what she was thinking? "Mine aren't for sale. Come on." Leading him by the hand, she showed him the rest of the house. She tried to get Devin talking, but he seemed far more interested in watching her move, the attention making her feel very, very special, if slightly shy.

Her house was larger than it looked from outside, Devin noticed, and was unusually furnished. Some rooms were a pleasant blend of styles, others totally given over to one particular era or culture. Some were light and airy, others dark and mysterious; all seemed to reflect her own changeable moods. Indeed, Bonnie seemed to change before his eyes, like a chameleon, depending on what room they were in. He watched and listened in utter fascination.

A sitting room with a predominantly Victorian theme made her seem prim and proper—her attire lending a subtle undertone of suppressed sensuality. The living room with an oriental decor made her irresistibly exotic; the modern oak and leather study gave her a distinct contemporary air. Her workroom, where she stored her magical apparatus and practiced, had a definite Gothic feeling with its rough-cut stone walls and intricate tapestries depicting mythic scenes.

Here more than anyplace else Devin felt he was seeing the real Bonnie Tyson: Confident, beguiling, somewhat aloof, with a now familiar, but still quite startling, aura of mystery, which he found at once exciting and forbidding. This was how she had seemed the first time he saw her, and he realized, rather uneasily, that this air of suspenseful mystery he felt uncomfortable with was the very thing about Bonnie that attracted him the most.

"What would you say if I told you I find you completely and totally fascinating?" he asked in a near whisper, taking her hands in his.

Bonnie smiled enigmatically. "I'd say my mother's salad dressing works quite well," she answered with a throaty laugh.

"You're impossible."

"I thought you said I was fascinating."

Devin pulled her close to him, looking into those eyes he couldn't seem to get enough of. "Impossibly fascinating." He kissed her, his tongue delicately outlining her full lips before plunging between them, feverishly seeking her equally willing tongue. "I think the oysters are working too."

His arousal was undeniable, and Bonnie didn't try to ignore it. She reveled in the erotic feel of him pressing against the soft swell of her stomach, once again within a touch of abandoning her objective. "I don't think you needed them," she teased, her mind swimming in a desire so strong she clung to Devin to keep from drowning.

"They were delicious. And so are you." He moaned as he took possession of her mouth once more. But again he sensed a certain hesitancy on her part. Had the thought been planted in his head? He pulled back to look at her and saw only desire. A frown of puzzlement wrinkled his brow. "Are you traipsing around in my mind again?" he asked jokingly, though an uneasy part of him wasn't laughing.

The corners of his mouth were lifted in a smile, but something in his eyes disconcerted her. "Not that I know of," she replied seriously.

His brow furrowed deeper. Was he going crazy? "Is something wrong?"

"Wrong? No, I—" Oh, damn it! What was the use? Whether he was truly aware of it or not, and whether she had allowed it to happen or not, Devin obviously sensed her change of mood. She couldn't say that she was hesitant exactly, she wanted him too much to say that. She was really more curious than anything, and she wasn't about to let her curiosity spoil this evening! "It's nothing really," she tried to reassure him, and herself. "It's just that . . . I . . ."

"What?"

Oh, hell! "It's really none of my business." She looked away, feeling incredibly foolish.

"Bonnie, tell me," he demanded softly. "If I'm pushing too fast, I'm sorry. I admit to being overwhelmed by you. I just thought the feeling was mutual. I feel . . . very strongly about you," he finished, running his hand through her hair.

"No! The feeling *is* mutual, Devin," she assured him, tilting her head to meet his warm gaze. She laughed at herself, glad when he stopped frowning and smiled with her. "This is silly. I just wanted to tell you I met your daughter earlier outside the clinic." There.

She had told him. The world hadn't ended, though he did look quite startled.

"You met Megan?"

"I told you it was silly." It was embarrassing to have behaved so foolishly about this. Bonnie wasn't about to add to her embarrassment by telling Devin how she and Megan had met. What reason did she have for jealousy at this stage of their relationship? She didn't own him. She was beginning to think she wanted to, but she wasn't completely sure—not yet. "We . . . bumped into each other as she was leaving. She recognized me, and I naturally found her face somewhat familiar too," Bonnie said, reaching a hand out to stroke his firm chin. "We talked a bit and—"

"Why?" His demand was not soft this time but harsh.

His tone startled her. What had come over him? Before he had worn a frown of concern, now it was a frown of anger. "Why what?" she asked in utter confusion.

"Why did she recognize you? Had she seen you before?" He released her and stepped back, his eyes intent on her face.

"Well, professionally. But—"

"What the hell does that mean?" he interrupted.

"What do you think it means?" she shot back, hands on her hips. She didn't like his tone at all and felt anger building within her. "She's seen me perform. I'm not totally unknown, you know."

"Oh." Devin's anger seemed to fade, but he was still looking at her with suspicion. "What did you talk about?"

"What is this, an inquisition?"

"Tell me!" he demanded.

"For heaven's sake, Devin, what's wrong with you?" Bonnie asked, bewildered by his desperation and angered by his demands. "We introduced ourselves and chatted for a moment. She had to leave and I was late to pick you up, so that was all. She seems like a very nice girl!" Bonnie finished in a tone that implied she was beginning to wonder whether her father was nice or not.

Devin sighed heavily, running his hands over his face in obvious exasperation. "I'm sorry. I just thought—"

"Thought what?" It was her turn to be demanding.

"Never mind. It doesn't matter. I'm sorry," he said contritely, stepping back to her and starting to pull her into his arms.

Bonnie pulled away. She was having none of it. "The hell it doesn't! Something had you nearly frantic for a moment there. What?"

"When you said Megan recognized you, I thought . . . Damn!" he finished in a mutter. "I thought perhaps she had consulted you," he blurted out. "But I was wrong. Let's just forget it." He looked at her, his eyes warm again, his voice full of sensuality when he said, "You still have a room left to show me, remember?"

Even as he spoke Bonnie saw by the look on his face that he seriously doubted he would get to see her bedroom, at least that evening. He was right. Bright spots of color appeared on her high cheekbones, evidence of the storm brewing inside her. "Why don't you ask me, Devin? I know the questions in your mind."

There it was, that strange gleam in her eyes. "Bonnie—"

"Then I'll just go ahead and answer them, shall I?" She clenched her teeth as she spoke. "No, I don't read tea leaves. I don't tell fortunes with cards. I don't talk with spirits of the dead, and I *don't* do consultations!" Her voice grew louder, and she paced in agitation. "I do, on occasion, talk to people, help my friends, and give advice to those who ask. When I do I behave like any other normal human being—which I am—without looking at sheep entrails or going into a trance! I'm a magician, not a medium. Consultations indeed!"

"Bonnie, please. You don't understand," Devin said. His voice held only a hint of the desperation he was feeling. "Megan is a very impressionable girl. I'm very protective of her."

He was trying to smooth her ruffled feathers, but his efforts were having just the opposite effect. "And you thought she'd need protecting from me?" Bonnie exploded in outrage. "What a flattering opinion of me you must have!" She cursed herself. She had allowed her attraction to Devin to blind her to her first impression of him, an obviously true impression. He *did* view her with distrust, *did* consider her an opportunistic charlatan. She shouldn't have allowed things to go this far, allowed herself to get so involved.

"I didn't know what to think. I didn't know how much of that mumbo jumbo you really believed," Devin replied irritably. "Megan is very susceptible to that kind of thing."

"Mumbo jumbo!" she exclaimed heatedly. "I'm the Magnificent Tyson, magician, not Madame Tyson the mystic palm reader!" The way she felt right now, she would trade all her skill as a magician for one good curse that really worked. Then the implications of what he was saying hit her—all his disapproval over her hospital visits, all his secretive behavior about his daughter. "Oh, I see! You were prepared to risk associating with me, but to allow me to associate with Megan is something else again, right?"

Devin looked startled—and furious. "And you think *I'm* paranoid! I should have known you had some kind of persecution complex by that display of self-righteousness at the hospital!"

Well. He had certainly hurt her with that one. "I think the bloom has gone out of this evening," she stated sarcastically.

"I said I was wrong. What more can I say?" he asked with a shrug of his broad shoulders.

Bonnie stopped her agitated pacing and glared at him. "I think all there is left to say is good night!"

Devin straightened, visibly irked. "If that's the way you feel. Good night!" He turned to leave but stopped, his back to her. "I haven't got a car," he said, positively beside himself with anger and frustration.

"I could give you a ride on my broom," she replied sweetly. "If you're not afraid I'll try to pop you into my oven," she added, cackling in her best impersonation of the Wicked Witch of the West.

She couldn't be sure if Devin's body shook with laughter or fury, and he didn't give her the chance to find out. "I'll walk!" he shot back in a strangled voice. "I could use the cool air!"

She watched him stomp out of her workroom, heard the slam of the front door. Yes, she thought, the cool air would do him good. As for herself, she'd choose a cool shower.

CHAPTER FOUR

Walking home was hardly the conclusion Devin had had in mind for the evening. Thoughts of a romantic dinner with Bonnie had made it difficult for him to concentrate all afternoon. But the same uncharacteristic lack of concentration had plagued him since he had met the mysterious Miss Tyson, so why should today have been any different?

It was a typical Colorado summer evening, with bright points of starlight in a cloudless sky and a soft quality to the air as Devin made his way home. Under the elm and oak trees lining the road the air was cooler, slightly humid. The silence of the night was broken by the gentle rustle of their leaves and the crunch of his shoes on the gravel shoulder. There were no sidewalks—probably never would be—for although this was a residential area, it was definitely *not* the suburbs. The road was paved now, but Devin clearly remembered a time when it was not. At sixteen, he had driven this road many times in his first car, an open-topped MG, thrilling to the feel of its wheels sliding on treacherous gravel. That had been before the house that was now his had even been built, before he had imagined he might live in this exclusive neighborhood, before his future had caught up with him and brought so many changes to his life—changes both wonderful and agonizingly painful.

A car went by on its way to the canyon road, and Devin caught the sound of youthful laughter, male and female. Time passed, but how little things really changed, he thought. "Don't get into trouble," he said with a wry smile, more to himself than to the teen-aged occupants of the passing car. They couldn't hear him. Even if they could, they wouldn't have listened. He hadn't at their age either. And in some ways he was very glad he hadn't. Pulling his thoughts away from the past, he walked on. He was thinking about Bonnie.

Perhaps he should have turned to her instead of walking out, showed her that he had been holding laughter in, not rage. But she was right. The bloom had gone out of the evening by then anyway, and he needed this time to sort out his feelings about her. It wasn't an easy task.

Devin couldn't for the life of him understand how he could be so fascinated by Bonnie—and that fascination, he noted, had progressed far beyond his original curiosity. Her philosophy of life couldn't be any more different from his own. As a man of science, he should scoff at her mysterious presence, her unquestioning optimism. Even her profession was the opposite of his own, he thought as he crossed a bridge spanning the boisterous creek alongside the road.

Magic and medicine used to be closely allied in the dim history of mankind, but as medicine progressed

71

beyond incantations and bloodletting with leeches, magic was put in its proper category, as simple showmanship or silly superstition. And yet, with Bonnie, Devin couldn't scoff. She was so obviously a serious professional. Her reaction to his implication that she might be a fortune-teller certainly put him in his place! He could still feel her outrage, see the defiance flashing in those magnificent eyes. Had he even detected a distaste in her voice for that kind of charlatan behavior he so disliked?

There was certainly nothing magical about the way he felt when close to her, or at least not in the manner of spells and love potions. He preferred to think of his attraction to her in terms of chemistry, or perhaps electricity: sparks certainly flew whenever they were together. No, the fact that they were drawn to each other was just that, a fact, not an illusion. They did tend to argue, but their arguments were really philosophical discussions, and Bonnie seemed to enjoy them as much as he did. So, in spite of their differences, he liked her. He only wished he knew her as well as she appeared to know him.

With a start Devin realized he was standing before his house. He went to the front door and let himself in, the emptiness of the place very noticeable after the delightful—if loudly interrupted—evening.

Bonnie's habit of answering questions he hadn't even asked yet was not only irritating, it was frustrating, and the real reason he had left so abruptly. It was eerie talking with someone who seemed to know his thoughts. He wanted to continue seeing her, whatever it meant in terms of personality clashes, but damn it!

Bonnie had a part of *his* concrete, rational mind half convinced she had magical powers, and mad as it made her, he really was concerned about her having any contact with Megan. What might her mysterious influence do to his impressionable young daughter?

"He called you a what!" Marcie exclaimed, trying, but not quite managing, to control her laughter.

"Well, he didn't actually say it in so many words," Bonnie admitted, "but he implied that I was some kind of back-room spiritualist or something."

"Was the evening going okay till then?" Marcie had inquired about her boss's date with Devin, expecting juicy details, not blow-by-blow descriptions of an argument.

"Very okay," Bonnie remarked, giving her assistant a lopsided grin. "Then I mentioned meeting his daughter, Megan, and he hit the ceiling! I got the distinct impression he feels I'm some sort of threat to her."

Marcie's eyes widened. "Why on earth would he think that? You're the sweetest person I know."

"You just say that because I pay your salary."

"But you do it so sweetly," Marcie replied, finally letting her laughter out.

The pair were busy refilling jars from large bags of supplies stored at the rear of the shop. Bonnie shot Marcie a skeptical glance as she returned one of the herb-filled jars to its proper place. "Anyway, Devin wasn't forthcoming with any information, though I suppose I am sort of at fault for that. I joined him on the ceiling when he started throwing innuendos

73

around, and there was more yelling than talking from that point on."

"Such as?" If she couldn't get any vicarious thrills, Marcie decided, she might as well hear about the argument.

"Oh, I don't know," Bonnie muttered. "We just have different views of the world, I guess."

"But you like him, right?"

That was an understatement. "Yes, I do. And I'm pretty sure he likes me. We're still leery of each other, that's all." But there *was* something else, something oddly secretive in Devin's behavior when it came to his daughter. "I sure would like to know why he's so protective of Megan, though," Bonnie added. "In fact, I'd like to know more about Megan, period."

"Didn't even get that far, huh?" Marcie asked.

"No. He's opinionated, and so am I. I flew off the handle when he implied I was a spiritual consultant of some kind. I don't know why people insist on thinking of magicians as possessing paranormal powers."

"You are a bit eerie at times," Marcie pointed out as tactfully as possible.

"I suppose," Bonnie agreed. "But I just wanted Devin to know I wasn't what he thought I was, and I told him so, perhaps a bit strongly."

"And he said?"

"He said I was paranoid. And I suppose I am to a certain extent, mainly because of him. He doesn't approve of my hospital visits, and no matter what he says, I still think he'd prefer it if I'd never met his daughter. It's a mystery," she finished with a perturbed sigh.

"And you," Marcie noted with sparkling eyes, "never could resist a good mystery."

They both went back to work, but Bonnie still turned the matter over in her mind. She freely admitted to a certain paranoia: throughout history magicians had been thought to possess paranormal powers, whether they themselves had encouraged the notion or not. Had she remained calm, she could have pointed out to Devin that it was a time-honored hobby among reputable magicians, escape artists, and stage mentalists to prove false the hoaxes perpetrated on an impressionable public by opportunistic spiritualists. Houdini had been a fanatic on the subject, exposing false mediums and seers with unequaled zeal. And yet Houdini himself had been branded as the possessor of true spiritual powers—no matter how many times he denied it. The superstitions surrounding him had served him well—after all, did they not help him to make a name for himself?—just as the air of mystery served all magicians well, including Bonnie herself. But now it was getting in her way.

Clearly, Devin didn't trust her around his daughter, and her own mysterious persona seemed to be the cause of his distrust. Well, she thought firmly, if she had to fight against some kind of absurd stereotype to win Devin, she would. She wasn't about to let *anything* come between them, not now, not when he had awakened such a fiery passion within her.

When lunchtime rolled around, Bonnie had decided to let tempers cool between her and Devin for a while, but she was still anxious to get to the bottom of this strange situation. A quick call to directory assistance got her Megan Warner's number. After all, she reasoned as she dialed the phone, Devin hadn't forbidden her to talk with Megan, he had only expressed concern over his daughter's impressionable nature. And, contrary to what Devin might think—given his overactive imagination—Bonnie wasn't looking for a soul to steal; she was looking for answers.

She didn't get many. Since Marcie had an afternoon class, Bonnie invited Megan to lunch at the small restaurant contained within the Victorian house, but they only had half an hour. It barely afforded them time for the most basic of pleasantries. She did discover, however, that her first impression of Megan had been correct. Devin's daughter was very nice and friendly, if slightly troubled for some reason. It rapidly became obvious to her that Megan would much rather talk about Bonnie than about herself or the past. Bonnie's sense of decorum prevented her from asking the questions that burned in her mind. If she had hoped for voluntary information, she found Megan even less forthcoming than Devin.

"How old are you, Megan?" It was the most straightforward question Bonnie had asked so far.

"Twenty. So you can see why Dad feels old." She laughed.

"Are you in school?" Perhaps her interests would shed some light on why Devin was so protective of her.

"Part-time at the community college. I'm looking for work now, but I was a typist at the college—in the sociology department. But that was before the budget cuts. How long have you been a magician?"

And so it went all during lunch, with Bonnie receiving small bits of information with a question about her own life tagged on the end. The only valuable, or at least promising, information came after lunch, when Bonnie invited Megan to see her shop.

"What courses do you take at the college?" she asked as she unlocked the cash register and prepared for the usual afternoon rush.

"Basics, mainly," Megan replied, looking around the shop with great interest. "I'm very interested in ancient history, though."

Bonnie laughed casually. "I'll have to introduce you to my parents. They're history buffs too. Myths and legends mostly."

"Me too!" she exclaimed. "I'm especially taken with the things I've read about your country."

"My country?" Bonnie asked, her brow furrowed in confusion.

"Yes, my father told me it was Tibet. Did you learn anything from the monks? I've heard they ve great powers and . . ." Her eyes were bright with excitement.

"I was only born there, Megan. I spent most of my childhood in Ohio when we weren't on the road."

"Oh."

"Sorry."

Megan laughed. "No, I'm sorry. Dad's always telling me I get too carried away with this junk."

It was the first time the sprightly brunette had come close to mentioning any probable cause for tension between herself and her father.

"It's not junk, Megan. There are many strange and

77

wonderful things in the world. Junk is probably your father's word for them, though."

They laughed together, Megan nodding in agreement. But just when Bonnie thought she might be close to gaining ground on the reason behind Devin's fit of the previous evening, Megan had to leave. At least she had opened the door for further discussions. Megan and she were rapidly becoming friends.

Though she hadn't gleaned much information from her conversation with Megan, Bonnie felt happy with what she had found out. She knew now that many of her assumptions had been correct. With Devin thirty-eight and his daughter twenty, he had indeed become a father at eighteen. Neither Megan nor her father was very talkative about the past, but that in itself told her something: Whatever had happened twenty years ago, it wasn't a comfortable subject for either of them, and out of respect for their feelings she would tread very lightly in that area from now on. And most important, she had learned that Megan was very interested in every aspect of the occult. So interested, as a matter of fact, that Bonnie could easily understand how Devin might interpret her interest as near obsession.

At home that evening Bonnie had just climbed into a soothing tubful of hot water, eager to think about all she had learned that day, when someone started pounding on her front door. She quickly toweled off; then, struggling into a fluffy blue terry-cloth robe, she went to see what insufferable clod was making such an incessant racket. It was Devin, and he looked angry.

His anger, however, wasn't sufficient to keep him from appreciating the woman who stood before him.

The sight of Bonnie in the short robe, with hair piled haphazardly on her head and the skin of her exposed thighs still pink from the hot bathwater, made him stop a moment and take it all in.

"Why, Devin," Bonnie remarked, enjoying his interested gaze, "what a surprise." It really *was* a surprise, though she had a pretty good idea what had brought him there.

"What's the matter? Have your antennae turned off this evening?" he asked, the sting of his sarcasm rendered considerably less effective by the sensual light in his eyes.

"Let's not start *that* again," Bonnie replied. "Come inside. I'm getting a chill standing here in the doorway."

Devin's gaze returned to her shapely bare legs. "Yes, I can see the goose bumps from here." He followed her to the living room, where she excused herself and went off to change.

In the long-sleeved floor-length caftan she wore when she returned, she felt much less at a disadvantage.

"Very nice," Devin said, obviously disappointed.

"Like it?" she asked, turning to give him the full—if less revealing—effect of the brightly colored garment. "I bought it in Marrakech. But then, I don't suppose you came here just to interrupt my bath and see a fashion show."

Devin's anger, temporarily held at bay by Bonnie's distracting appearance at the door, now returned full force. "No. I came to find out why you've been sneaking around behind my back." He spat the words out.

Bonnie took a seat opposite him, looking quite at ease in her cross-legged position on the tatami mat. "Whatever do you mean?"

"Don't goad me! You know damn well what I mean!"

When he wanted them to, Bonnie noticed calmly, Devin's blue eyes could look quite frosty. "If you're referring to my pleasant lunch with Megan, I'd hardly call that sneaking behind your back. She's an adult and perfectly free to choose her friends."

"Is that what you are?" he asked coolly.

His sarcasm was getting on her nerves. "No, I read her palm and told her fortune with chicken bones," she returned.

Devin muttered an expletive under his breath. "I wouldn't put it past you."

"Your delusions are your problem," she shot back. Bright spots of color had appeared on her cheeks, but she tried to remain calm. Trading snide comments hadn't gotten them anywhere the night before. "We ate, and talked, and had a very nice time. And yes, we are becoming friends."

"What did you talk about?" His words were spoken conversationally, but Bonnie felt the suspicion beneath them.

She looked heavenward and sighed deeply. "Give me strength." She leveled her gaze at Devin. "We chatted, talked. You know, held a normal conversation of the kind you and I seem incapable of sustaining for more than a few minutes at a time lately."

Rising from his perch on the black lacquered settee, Devin came around the low table between them and sank to the floor beside her. He looked into her eyes, giving her a chagrined smile. "I'm sorry. I've done it again, haven't I?"

"Done what?"

"Impugned your profession."

Bonnie chuckled pleasantly. "Yes, and I'll get you for it," she promised with a wicked grin. This was much better. She liked being close to him—had thought of very little else since his abrupt departure the night before. "Actually, Megan and I spent most of our time discussing just that—my profession."

His eyes narrowed slightly. "Oh?"

"You were right, she does seem impressionable, very ready to believe almost anything. I found her open-mindedness refreshing."

"I find it dangerous."

"Why?"

Devin's expression became guarded. "There are some things I wish didn't impress her quite so much," he answered quietly.

The occult was a rather dark and unusual interest for a twenty-year-old, but Bonnie would hardly call it dangerous. Though she wanted to press for more answers, the look on his face told her she wouldn't get them, or at least not easily. And the mood of the evening had changed to the point where Bonnie didn't want to argue anymore. Devin had calmed down and she wanted him to stay that way, for her own reasons. He looked so handsome that evening, dressed in gray slacks and matching sport coat, with a pale blue shirt open at the neck to display his tanned throat. Again she wanted to know just how far that tan went. Now, that was a promising question! "Would you like a drink?"

Devin shook his head. "I would, but I can't. I'm on call this evening."

"Tea, then?"

"Sounds good," he replied appreciatively.

Returning with a steaming pot of tea and small matching cups—their delicate hand-painted design was in perfect harmony with the tranquil oriental decor—Bonnie was in for a surprise. Devin, who in her absence had removed his shoes and coat, was now sitting cross-legged. His forearms, bared by rolled-up sleeves, were resting on his knees. He was breathing deeply, and his eyes were closed. They opened when Bonnie knelt beside him and poured the tea.

"With this room," he said softly, waving a hand at the oriental furnishings, "you should be wearing a kimono."

Bonnie smiled and handed him a cup of fragrant herb-and-fruit tea. "And this should be green tea, not chamomile. Culturally confused, that's me." She cocked her head at him curiously. "I hardly expected to find you meditating!"

Devin laughed, the fully relaxed laugh Bonnie loved to hear. "I don't chant or try to plumb the depths of my soul or anything, if that's what you mean. I just close my eyes and breathe," he explained. "It's very good for your blood pressure," he added in a serious tone, as if caught in an admission of guilt. "I've read studies in the medical journals."

"Uh-huh."

"It is!"

The look on Devin's face was very much like that of a friend of hers she had stumbled upon one day at a local burger joint. She had caught him, a health-food devotee, gobbling cheeseburgers and mountains of fries. "Your secret is safe with me," she assured him, breaking into peals of laughter at his indignant expression. "Who got you to try it?"

"Megan, actually," Devin replied, sipping his tea haughtily.

"I thought so. See? An open mind isn't that bad."

"Hmm." He didn't sound at all convinced.

"You two are very close, aren't you?"

He nodded, his face lighting up with a gentle smile. "Much closer than most fathers and daughters. I suppose that's why I worry so much about her." He turned to Bonnie, his hand reaching out to cover hers where it rested on her thigh. "I'm sorry if you're getting trampled under the clumsy feet of my protective zeal."

His touch sent a thrill through her, a thrill that immediately turned into a spreading warmth. Her voice was sultry when she spoke. "I really just wanted to know more about you, about your life. I didn't mean it to be underhanded in any way. I like Megan. She's the kind of person one can become very fond of in a very short time." Bonnie stroked the strong line of his jaw. "Just like her father."

Devin turned his face and kissed her caressing palm, feeling her shiver in delight when his tongue touched the sensitive skin. "You're quite easy to be fond of yourself," he murmured. He pulled her body to his, a startled moan of desire catching in her throat as he kissed her, parting her lips to plunder the sweet and willing mouth awaiting him.

There was no resistance in Bonnie now. She was rapidly being drawn beyond the point of caring about the secret Devin seemed to be keeping from her, the mystery of Megan. The only mystery she cared about tonight was the one of Devin's tan, and how much of his hard, well-muscled masculine form it covered. Her hands went to his shirt, slowly unbuttoning it to reveal his chest. So far, so good, her impassioned mind told her. She ran her hands over the defined contours of his skin, then slipped them around his sides to his back. She had waited long enough to feel the heat of his body underneath her fingers. Their tips now dug into his firm flesh and powerful muscle as desire coursed through her, a desire more primitive than she had ever believed possible.

Devin withdrew from her just far enough to glide his hand across her breasts, reveling in the shudder his caress brought from her. But the fabric of her caftan, though thin, was still too much interference for him. He wanted to mold her sweet breasts in his hands, feel the taut buds of her nipples against his palms. Before Bonnie's passion-clouded mind could remember the seemingly endless row of intricately woven buttons that would surely frustrate his delicious explorations, Devin's deft surgeon's hands had the caftan undone clear down to her stomach. She gasped in pleasure when his thumbs brushed the hardened peaks of her breasts. A liquid fire began to burn deep in the center of her being.

With gentle impatience he tugged the garment from

her shoulders and down over her arms, which, once freed, wrapped around his neck to pull him close once more. Their bodies pressed together intimately for the first time, skin to skin, bringing a mutual sigh of satisfaction to their lips. Bonnie lay back on the soft mat beneath them, Devin following, deepening his kiss.

"Those buttons were supposed to be a formidable barrier," she taunted, whispering in his ear as he nibbled lightly at her neck, his tongue driving her wild with its lingering trail of fire.

"They failed," he murmured in return. "I'm glad you trusted them so much. There certainly aren't any other barriers to be found." He emphasized the point with his hand, gliding it down across her stomach, over her hip, underneath the caftan to her thigh, encountering nothing but smooth, feverishly warm skin. "None at all." His voice was a sensual whisper.

She, too, was impatient to get on with her quest. He helped her remove his shirt, and she now saw that his tan didn't stop anywhere on his lean torso, but she still wasn't satisfied. Her hands dipped to the waistband of his slacks, feeling the muscles of his flat stomach tighten at her feathery touch. Her quest was momentarily forgotten, however, when Devin's lips and tongue continued on their relentless journey, greedily plundering every sensitive inch of her breasts. He nuzzled the smooth underside of each one before pulling its exquisitely hard nipple into his mouth, his tongue drawing maddening circles around it.

"Oh, God, Devin. I . . ." She moaned, her body arching to his.

His lips returned to hers, his eyes sparkling mischievously. "Sweet Bonnie, I want you too. That is what you wanted to say, isn't it?" His voice was hoarse, sensually deep.

She nodded, suddenly shy, and pressed her face against his broad chest. Her shyness disappeared as quickly as it had come. Her tongue found and circled his nipple, drawing a startlingly strong response from him, a response she definitely wanted to feel and hear more of. Once again her hand found the button of his slacks, but just as she was about to end her quest by revealing the extent of his tan, the phone rang.

"Oh, hell!" Devin muttered.

"Another salesman," Bonnie murmured. His hand had begun a delightfully promising path along her inner thigh. Why had he stopped? "Ignore it."

His expression told her he was sorely tempted to, but his voice told of his frustration and resignation. "Damn! I can't. I'm on call tonight, remember? I gave this number when I left the clinic. They know I can be reached for a while. It could be an emergency."

Bonnie had admired his dedication before, but she didn't think much of it at the moment. She got up and slipped her arms back into the caftan, then went to answer the phone. "Maybe it's a wrong number," she mumbled hopefully.

It wasn't. It was for Devin, and apparently an emergency. She saw his magnificent back muscles tense as he spoke into the phone in short, clipped sentences. When he hung up he turned, giving Bonnie a desperate glance that would have been humorous in other circumstances. It was quite obvious he didn't want to leave, but just as obvious he had to.

"What happened?"

"Industrial accident. I'll spare you the details."

"I appreciate that." The thought alone made Bonnie shudder.

He pulled his shirt on, slipped into his shoes, and grabbed his coat; then he pulled her into an embrace that nearly took her breath away with its undercurrent of frustrated desire. "Call you tomorrow?" he asked, his hands slipping inside the still-unbuttoned caftan to press against the small of her back.

"If you don't, you'd better believe I'll call you!" she promised breathlessly.

He gave her a roguish grin that made her feel warm from head to toe, and then he was gone.

Damn! Not only had a by now familiar ache returned, but she hadn't even found out if he had a tan-line! Nor had she come any closer to unraveling the other mystery, the secrets yet to be revealed to her. Both Warners were closemouthed about the past. And every time she thought she was getting close, either Megan changed the subject, or Devin seduced her—or she him. Oh, well, she thought, smiling happily and shivering at the memory of his skillful touch. You can't have everything.

CHAPTER FIVE

"I don't think I want to hear this," Bonnie said when she saw the nervous, somewhat sorrowful expression on Marcie's face the next morning.

"I don't really want to say it," Marcie replied.

Bonnie sighed, poured herself a cup of tea, and sat down at the table in the back room of the shop. "Quit fidgeting and tell me."

Marcie joined her at the table. "I have a chance at an entry-level management position with a solar technology firm in Fort Collins. I know it's short notice, but I'm pretty sure I've got the job. I told you I was sending out feelers last month."

"Yes, I know. I've been expecting this, Marcie. You're too sharp and too ambitious to remain a clerk in a tea shop the rest of your life." Bonnie could tell Marcie was upset about leaving her in the lurch, but they had known each other too long for her to miss the excitement in her assistant's voice. It was a big break, one Marcie had worked hard for, and Bonnie certainly wasn't going to stand in her way. Still, she found it hard to ask the question she knew she had to ask. "How soon . . ."

"I'm driving up there for an appointment this morning," Marcie supplied. "If things work out like I expect them to, they'll want me to start at the beginning of next week. Of course, today's Wednesday, and I'll need to find a place, and I want to register for night school and—"

Bonnie leaned over and hugged her. "Whatever you need to do, do," she said reassuringly. "Go for it." Giving her a big pat on the back, she released Marcie and beamed at her. "I'm so proud of you!"

"And I'm so sorry. I know you're coming into your busy season with the magic act, and you'll have to find a replacement for me here. I feel like a traitor!"

"Nonsense! Like I said, I've been expecting this. As long as you promise not to be a stranger. And please, please tell me I can call you up if I have any business questions."

Thus reassured, Marcie could feel happiness break through her anxiety. "Anytime. You'll do fine, though." She polished her nails on her shirtfront in a gesture of self-mocking pride. "After all, I taught you everything I know."

"Hardly," Bonnie returned, laughing at the uncharacteristic display of egotism. "But speaking of knowledge, you will keep practicing your magic, won't you?"

Marcie nodded her promise. "Say, I know a couple of women at school who might be interested in working here. Want me to get in touch with them?" she asked.

An idea was forming in Bonnie's mind, an idea that would undoubtedly get her into trouble with Devin, but one she couldn't let loose once it struck her. "You might give me their names and numbers just in case." She smiled enigmatically. "But I think I already have someone in mind who would work out very nicely here."

Marcie's news was upsetting, mainly because of the comfortable routine Bonnie had grown accustomed to. But the really upsetting news came a bit later when Bonnie finally got the call she had been waiting for. Devin was going to Boston for three days to fill in for one of his partners at the clinic who had suddenly fallen ill. Evidently he was going to be teaching a group of medical students about the use of laser beams in eye surgery.

"What's a YAG laser?" she asked glumly, knowing he had to catch a plane soon, but unwilling to stop listening to his voice just yet. "I know a laser is a concentrated beam of light, but YAG sounds like what you'd say when you've got something stuck in your throat."

"Yttrium aluminum garnet," he answered.

"Oh. That explains everything."

Devin laughed, Bonnie loving the sound. "It creates a very intense beam, twenty-seven thousand degrees at a power level of ten million watts."

"I see."

"The beam can be used something like a scalpel."

"Uh-huh. And you call me a mystic."

She could almost hear his smile. "I really do have to go," Devin said gently.

"I know." She sighed. "I hope your students appreciate you as much as I do."

"Even the female ones?" he taunted.

"Just keep in mind, buster, how silly you'd look without your ears! When will you be back?" It wouldn't be soon enough.

"Let's see." There was a pause. "I arrive here at seven Saturday night."

"I'll have dinner ready at my house."

"And the phone off the hook?"

"Definitely. Oh, and Devin? I want to . . ." Her voice trailed off. Should she tell him about wanting to hire Megan? No, she didn't even know if Megan would want the job.

"Yes?" he asked.

"Nothing. It can wait till Saturday night."

"I don't know if I can," he said with a voice so warm it sent a shiver up Bonnie's spine, even over the phone. "See you then."

Since she had given Marcie leave to do whatever was necessary to procure the new job and get settled in Fort Collins, Bonnie was now on her own with the shop. Wednesday was normally Marcie's day off, so she had planned on working today anyway, and Thursday and Friday were no problem. Saturday, however, was one of Marcie's full days, and this coming Saturday Bonnie had promised to perform at a local hospital. So if she was going to hire and train someone, she had better get started immediately.

When Bonnie approached her with the offer of a job, Megan not only wanted it but jumped at the chance. Luckily, she knew how to handle a cash register, having served a short stint at the campus bookstore, and at the end of her first day was weighing and measuring herbs and grinding coffee like an old pro.

When they closed up that night, Bonnie was very pleased with her new helper. With Megan's willowy good looks and friendly attitude it seemed they wouldn't even lose the young male trade Marcie had attracted. "You're going to work out fine, Megan," Bonnie assured her. "I'll help you tomorrow and Friday, and part of Saturday, but I think you'll be well able to handle the place a full day on your own sometime next week. We'll sit down and work out a schedule on Monday."

Megan, blue eyes sparkling, was very pleased as well. "I love working here already. It's fun, so much better than secretarial work. I can use the money too!"

"Does Devin help you out with tuition and such?" Bonnie wondered out loud, not meaning to pry.

"Help me out! He covers it all, rent too."

Bonnie thought she detected something in Megan's voice. Not resentment, but slight irritation perhaps. "How do you feel about that?"

Megan chuckled, responding with an honesty that was typical of her. "Oh, I appreciate it. He's giving me time to sort myself out, and he's very patient. A bit overprotective, though," she added wryly.

"So I've noticed," Bonnie muttered.

"Hmm?"

She wanted to know more, but subtle was better than direct in this case. "How about dinner to celebrate your new job?" Bonnie asked, changing the subject.

Megan's heart-shaped face usually held an expression of youthful innocence, but now her expression turned evasive. "I, uh, have an appointment this evening. Maybe tomorrow?"

The evasiveness disappeared as quickly as it had come, making Bonnie wonder if it had been there at all. Still, she had said appointment, not date, and she had spoken with an odd hesitancy. Was Devin so protective because there was something suspicious going on in Megan's life? Bonnie stopped herself with a mental jerk. Good grief! she thought. I sound just like Devin! Talk about being suspicious and overprotective. "Okay. See you tomorrow after your morning classes, then?"

"I'll be here," Megan promised.

As Bonnie watched her hasty departure she started wondering once more: Why was Megan in such a hurry? And if Devin covered all her expenses, why did she seem in need of money?

Stop it! she scolded herself again. Maybe Megan did have a date and simply hadn't wanted to tell her for fear she in turn might tell Devin. Bonnie had been the same way with her own father, not wanting him to put her through the third degree every time she went out —something Devin himself was probably very good at doing. And maybe Megan wanted to earn money she could call her own, even though Devin undoubtedly supported her with no strings attached.

And maybe pigs fly, Bonnie thought finally. Her suspicions might be unfounded, but they were very real to her nonetheless.

Saturday afternoon Bonnie was no closer to finding any real basis for her suspicions—but no closer to shaking them either. Megan and she were very friendly now, and she felt instinctively that they trusted each other well enough for Megan to tell her about any men in her life without fear of its getting back to Devin. But Megan didn't say a word about her mysterious appointment Wednesday evening, and had even run off to another on Friday, giving the same evasive and hesitant explanation.

As the time to close up shop rolled around, though, Bonnie ceased to think about secrets. Her thoughts turned completely to the subject that had scarcely been out of her mind for the last four days—Devin. He was due in at seven, would probably be at her house by eight, and she still had to go home, get ready, and prepare the rock lobster tails and sirloin steak she had planned for their dinner.

Excited and preoccupied, she didn't realize she had forgotten to lock the door before settling down to total the day's receipts until she heard it open. "I'm sorry, we're closed," she said without looking up, so anxious was she to finish the job quickly.

"Your money or your . . ." a male voice demanded.

Startled, Bonnie did look up, right into Devin's eyes. "My money or my what?" she asked, running her tongue over her lips in sensual invitation.

"I'm thinking," he replied wickedly.

"You need to think?" She came around the counter, trying not to look as anxious as she felt. "My spell must be wearing off."

"Mmm. Trying to decide what I want the most." Wrapping his arms around her and nearly lifting her off the ground, he made the decision: "A kiss, I do believe, at least in these public surroundings."

How good it felt to be in his arms! And how good his lips tasted as they pressed against hers, his tongue parting them with a demand Bonnie gladly met. Her hands went to his neck, holding him, not wanting the kiss to end. His hands found the small of her back and pulled her against his hips, communicating his need.

Devin groaned and released her, looking into her eyes. "I'll take a dozen more of those, to go, if you please."

"I'm almost finished here," she promised, a bit dazed.

"Well, hurry. I—" He stopped, looking over her shoulder.

Megan emerged from the back room, where she had been running an inventory on a newly arrived shipment of coffee. "What's going on here?" she asked with a tentative grin.

Devin looked at his daughter, then back at Bonnie. His eyes narrowed. "Now, there's a good question."

"Marcie got a job in Fort Collins, and when I remembered Megan was looking for work, I asked her to come to work for me. She agreed," Bonnie explained, her tone a bit more defiant than she had intended. She couldn't help it. She knew Devin's angry look when she saw it.

"I see," he replied simply, obviously at a loss as to how to handle the situation. He was, however, staring at Bonnie, a disapproving look on his face.

"I really like it here, Dad. Bonnie's a wonderful boss."

Noting the element of defiance in Megan's voice, too, Bonnie felt a certain camaraderie. "And Megan is a wonderful employee."

Devin turned his gaze to Megan, the tight lines around his mouth relaxing into a tender smile. She did look happy, happier than he had seen her in a while. "I can see where you two would get along well together," he said at last. "You're a lot alike." He refrained from saying why he thought so. It wasn't just their shared interests, or their wide-open minds. They were both rebellious as well. He knew there wasn't a lot he could do about this development other than accept it.

Bonnie relaxed, and Megan, she saw, had done the same. "She's really taken to the job, that's for sure. She's a real godsend."

"I always thought so too," Devin agreed.

Megan rewarded him with a bright smile and a hug. "Well, I know you two have a date tonight, and I have to study for a math test on Monday, so I guess we all better get out of here. Good night." She waved on her way out the door.

"When did you hire her?" Devin asked when she was gone.

He wasn't angry anymore, but Bonnie could tell he was perturbed. "Um, the day after you left, actually," she replied hesitantly. "I was going to tell you tonight, over dinner, just in case she didn't work out."

Devin tried but couldn't keep from smiling. "Ah-hah! So the dinner was to pacify me, I suppose."

Bonnie stepped closer and put her arms around him, opening her eyes wide. "Among other things. Of course, if you'd rather not come . . ."

Devin grabbed her before she could slip away. "Shall I follow you right now?"

"No, I have a bank deposit to make, then I need time to get ready, and to cook dinner. You weren't even supposed to be in town for another hour yet."

"I got an early flight. Besides, I thought *you* were the main course," Devin replied rakishly.

"Devin!"

He squeezed, then released her. "I'll give you the time to get ready. I could use a shower myself. But we'll cook dinner together. Okay?"

"Okay."

An hour later they were side by side in Bonnie's kitchen, drinking white wine and fixing a salad. Devin had cut the shells of the lobster tails and basted the tender white meat with butter before putting them under the broiler. Bonnie had set a lovely table out on her patio, where two steaks sizzled on a hibachi.

Finally everything was ready, and they sat down to eat surrounded by the sound of crickets, caressed by a soft warm breeze. An ornate kerosene lamp bathed them in mellow light. Bonnie had decided on black cotton pants—not tight, but close fitting enough to show off her figure—and a white lace blouse with a daring décolletage. Devin looked very relaxed and handsome in gray slacks and a pale blue knit shirt. His shirt, she noticed with amusement, had a small alligator with its feet in the air instead of the usual trendy reptile.

"I like it here," Devin said with a sigh. "Seems more like a home than my own."

Bonnie dipped a morsel of her lobster into a spicy seafood sauce, disdaining the butter. "With your life-style I imagine you aren't there enough for it to seem like home."

"True." He laughed ruefully. "Believe it or not, though, I've slowed down in the last year."

Bonnie thought of his booming practice, his lectures, his trips to far cities to teach or consult. "You must have been killing yourself," she observed.

Devin nodded. "That's what I finally decided. I'd like to slow down even more, really. Fewer seminars, fewer new patients. Maybe write a few papers or even a book." His expression turned thoughtful. "I really enjoyed this last trip, the teaching part. It would be nice to do more of that."

"It sounds," Bonnie replied, laughing gently, "as if that's more work, not less."

Devin joined in her laughter. "I guess you're right."

"You really like your work, don't you?"

"Yes. It's all I've ever wanted to do. I suppose you can say the same thing, can't you?" he asked, pouring them both another glass of wine.

"I suppose. I was born into it really, and I inherited the knack. It's nice to be successful at something that comes easily to you, and if you enjoy what you do as well, it's an added bonus."

Devin had put his hand over hers, his smile warm and relaxed. "Why is it you don't travel anymore? I mean, I notice you don't run off to do shows in Las Vegas and that sort of thing."

"It's just that I got so tired of performing for Las Vegas–type crowds. I've spent almost eighteen years of my life directly or indirectly involved in that kind of rat race, long enough to decide it's not for me," she explained. "I enjoy the stage shows I do for benefits, but I found my real calling in the shows I do for the children." She knew this was a sore subject with Devin, but they were getting very close—and with any luck would get still closer—and she wanted to get it out in the open. Her hospital performances were a very enjoyable and important part of her life.

Devin did get a slightly dismayed look on his face. "I'm still not sure how I feel about that," he said doubtfully. "I mean, I'm willing to admit I over-reacted at the hospital. I don't think you do the kids any harm. But—"

"But you don't think I'm doing them any good either, right?"

"Well . . ."

Taking his hand, Bonnie got up. "Come on," she requested. "I want to show you something."

Devin let her lead him back into the house, where they went to her workroom. She had him sit in a chair before a makeshift stage, then dimmed the light cast by an overhead chandelier.

"How do you feel?" she asked from the stage.

"Fine."

Bonnie laughed at his amused tone. "No, I mean *what* do you feel?"

"Oh, I see." He thought for a moment. "If you must know, I suppose I feel a bit eerie. The dim light, these

Gothic surroundings." He waved a hand—a gesture that spoke of the mystical decor of her workroom.

She moved to a table draped with black lace, reached beneath it, and produced four spheres, their surfaces iridescent in the low light. Manipulating them from hand to hand, she increased, then decreased their number, until only one was left. Holding the remaining sphere between thumb and forefinger, she lifted her hand for Devin to see it.

He smiled appreciatively. "How do you do that?"

"We magicians have a stock answer for that question," she replied. "I do it very well." She laughed at his rueful sigh. "That's what is known as sleight of hand. It takes skill, dexterity, lots of practice, and more than a little bit of talent to do really well."

"Then the answer fits," he admitted. "You do it very well indeed."

"Thank you. Now how do you feel?"

"Well, mystified I suppose."

With a flourish she threw the ball at him, but it disappeared in a flash of flame and a puff of smoke. "And now?" she asked again.

It had happened so quickly Devin didn't have time to watch, only react. He nearly fell out of his chair. Clearing his throat nervously, he replied, "Still mystified, but with a difference. That gave me a real shot of adrenaline, my heart's still pounding. I hope you don't do that for children. It's dangerous." His tone was scolding.

"Not in trained hands, but no, I don't do that for children. You may not admit it, but you were frightened for an instant. I helped to prepare your mind for this with the dim lighting. I don't frighten hospital patients of any age. Now," she said, turning up the lights and coming over to his chair, "this is what I do for children."

Devin watched, entranced by her movements as she released the chignon at the back of her head, letting her hair fall to flow freely. She reached into her pocket and brought out a small silver box, handing it to him with its hinged lid open. "I'm tempted to say it's empty," he said, looking inside. "But knowing you, I'll withhold judgment."

Bonnie took the box back, smiled mysteriously, then turned around once, her hair a swirling curtain. Facing him, she held the box cradled in her hands, tapping the top with one fingertip. "Hello in there!" she called.

Slowly the lid to the box opened, seemingly by itself, and a tiny handkerchief rabbit poked its way out, first its ears, then its head, and finally two little cloth paws. It looked around with small painted eyes, wriggled its pink nose, then recoiled in surprise when it saw Devin. One paw reached up and grabbed the box lid, closing it with a snap as the rabbit sank quickly out of sight.

Devin blinked, looked up at Bonnie, and started laughing uproariously. With a flourish she handed him the box. It was empty. Startled, he started laughing all over again.

"Magic!" she whispered. "Though there's some sleight of hand involved, both the ball disappearing in flame and my little friend in the box are known as illusions, make-believe, but with entirely different purposes. Flames and smoke are to amaze, shock, even frighten to some extent. Harry the rabbit delights, amuses, creates a feeling of wonder," she explained, sitting down next to Devin. "You should hear the children laugh when they see him."

Still chuckling himself, Devin slowly nodded his head. "I think I understand. There's magic for adults, and magic for children."

"And magic for sick children," she added. "I don't perform in intensive-care units or recovery rooms. Laughter is good medicine, but not for abdominal or internal stitches. For a child with a broken leg or a young patient faced with a long stay in unfamiliar surroundings, though, my magic and the stuffed animals I hand out can make the difference between inconvenience and a very bad time."

"I owe you an apology," Devin said, reaching out to push an errant lock of hair behind her ear. "I didn't realize you were quite so involved in this sort of thing." Devin was seeing Bonnie in a new light. In her own way, with her unique skills, she was as dedicated to helping people as he was.

"Performing for the children or for civic benefits restored the sense of fulfillment I had lost after so many years on the road," Bonnie explained.

"Less demanding?" Devin asked.

She laughed softly. "In some ways the direction I've chosen is even *more* demanding, and I certainly have the same drive to develop and perfect my skills. The difference, I suppose, comes from the way I feel about my magic inside. It's not a job anymore, it's an art I practice to make people happy. What I do now is real magic."

Devin's brow furrowed. She wasn't going to start in again with the mumbo jumbo, was she? "Real magic?" he asked skeptically.

"With skill and training I perform illusions. They make people laugh and wonder, make them willing to suspend belief for just a little while in a world with too much harsh reality. The real magic," Bonnie continued softly, "is in the mind. And in the heart." She placed her hand on his chest for emphasis.

Her touch was deliciously warm over his heart. "I think, Miss Mysterious Tyson, that I'm finally beginning to understand you."

Bonnie leaned close and kissed him gently, feeling the spark of desire kindle between them. "That's real magic," she murmured. "How do you feel now?" It was a question she scarcely needed to ask. She could feel his answer beneath her hands, in the beating of his heart.

"I feel," Devin replied, his eyes alive with a sensual gleam, "like showing you some of my own brand of magic." Plucking her easily from her chair, he stood with her in his arms. "Levitation," he announced. Her arms around his neck, he carried her from the room and out into the hallway. "Teleportation," he explained throatily as he headed toward the one room in her house he had yet to see—her bedroom. "My vanishing act is a bit rusty, though, and my hands are full, so if you'd just open the door . . ."

Bonnie reluctantly took one hand from behind his neck and opened the door he now stood in front of, turning on the light as he carried her into the room.

He swung her around and closed the door with her outstretched legs. "And that was?" she asked huskily.

"Sleight of foot, of course."

"Of course."

Putting her lightly on her feet, Devin began unbuttoning her blouse slowly, taking great pleasure in revealing her pale skin inch by inch, his eyes aflame with desire. "Now, with your assistance, I intend to make all our clothes disappear," he said, his voice roughened by passion. "But first . . ." He reached over and unplugged her bedside phone. "Now nothing can save you."

Bonnie didn't want to be saved. She had a quest, a quest near its conclusion. With fingers that were sure despite her trembling desire, she pulled his shirt over his head, then ran her hands down his chest and hard stomach to the waistband of his slacks. At last, she thought, at last I'll find out how much he wears when he sunbathes!

But Devin had a quest also. Her blouse joined his shirt on the Persian rug beneath their feet, and his hands covered her breasts with a gentle, possessive caress that drew a delighted intake of breath from her lips. His touch was skilled, too, and just as fast, as he slid her black pants down her legs before she knew what was happening. His lips and tongue, too, followed a downward path along her thighs until she feared her knees would give way beneath her. Suddenly she was in his arms again as he picked her up and laid her on the bed, its sheer canopy diffusing the light to a warm glow. His eyes devoured her as she lay there wearing only her black lace panties, an inviting smile lighting her face.

And then she discovered that whatever he wore when sunbathing, it had to be quite brief. His legs were tanned to the tops of his thighs, as was his torso to just below the navel, the pale band between exciting by contrast and noticeably male—very noticeably. He stretched out beside her, and they embraced as if that alone could save them from the burning fire of passion coursing through their veins. But the contact of their bodies only made the fire burn hotter, demanding more fuel for the flames.

Bonnie's searching hands found the exciting pale skin of his buttocks, her fingertips digging deep into the powerful muscle. She gasped at the powerful erotic images flooding through her mind. Devin's tongue began an intricate path along her sides, pausing to tease each swelling breast. She cried out with joy. He moved on, down over her belly, to nibble lightly on her thighs, grazing her femininity in passing until she writhed beneath his touch. Just when she felt as if she would surely explode, his mouth returned to hers, his tongue plunging deep, its thrust demanding, nearly desperate.

Unable to hold his desire in check for a moment longer, Devin gently slid his powerful body between her sweet thighs, his impassioned mind swimming with the willing, equally desperate way Bonnie offered herself to him. She arched her hips to his welcome and expert thrust. The culmination of this long-awaited moment filled her with a joy so strong she cried out his name in happiness. They were still for a moment, gazing into each other's eyes, lost in the depths of the pleasurable sensation of oneness. Then they moved together, reveled in each other's pleasure, feverishly scaling peak after peak in search of the release too long denied them.

Bonnie moved with Devin's strong rhythm, marveling at the way their bodies fit, stunned by the perfection and symmetry they shared. It was as if they were made for each other, Devin the only man for her and she the only woman for him. Their mutual longing suspended them in time, held them loving captives in a truly magic world of pleasure given and joyously returned, until at last that desperate longing could no longer be denied: it now exploded over and through them with an intensity that left them breathless. They shared a freedom then, softly laughing together as they lay bathed in the tender afterglow, amazed they had lived through such intense feelings.

"Are we still alive?" Bonnie wondered breathlessly.

"Very much alive," Devin murmured softly. He gently brushed errant strands of silky hair from her face and kissed her. "I want to stay this way forever, just holding you in my arms."

"Mmm," Bonnie agreed. "Forever." Her heart was pounding—pounding in her ears, pounding so loudly . . .

"Oh, God." Devin groaned. "Now what?"

The fog slowly clearing from her mind, Bonnie realized it wasn't her heart that was making so much noise but someone at the front door. "They'll go away," she managed to murmur, though her breath was coming so fast, her voice was barely more than a whisper.

"Ms. Tyson? Are you all right?" a deep, masculine voice called from the back of the house.

The voice penetrated her delicious lethargy. "Oh, hell! I left the patio door open!" Bonnie cried.

"This is the police. Are you all right?" the voice called again, a bit louder, and a bit closer. He was coming up the hall!

With startled expressions Bonnie and Devin looked at each other, then jumped up and started dressing as fast as possible.

"I—I'm fine! Who's there?" Bonnie yelled, struggling into her blouse.

"Police! Is everything all right in there?" the voice asked, this time from outside the bedroom door.

Bonnie took a step backward, right onto Devin's toe. "Ouch!" he yelped.

"Are you sure you're all right?" The voice, which expressed a certain suspicion, was accompanied by a tentative knock.

Barely managing to contain a fit of near hysterical laughter at the absurdity of the situation, Bonnie opened the door. She found herself face to face with a patrolman who didn't look old enough to have such a deep voice.

"Ms. Tyson?"

"Yes?"

"I'm sorry to disturb you. There's been a break-in at your store. We tried to call, but your phone must be out of order."

Bonnie looked over her shoulder at Devin, who could do little more than shrug with a pained expression on his face.

The policeman seemed to notice him for the first time. His eyes went from Bonnie to Devin, then back to Bonnie. His face had an unusual expression. "Anyway, when we got here, your back door was wide open. Sometimes a burglar will rob a place of business and get the keys and address of the owner's place of residence, which he or she proceeds to rob as well. We thought you might be in need of assistance and—"

"Did you find her, Chuck?" A second uniformed officer appeared in the doorway, cutting off his younger partner's speech. He, too, gave Devin and Bonnie a strange look. Then his eyebrows arched, and he turned abruptly to leave. "Oops. Come on, Chuck. We'll wait for you outside, Ms. Tyson." Chuck shut the door, and they could hear the two policemen having a heated discussion all the way down the hall.

Bonnie turned to Devin, then burst out laughing despite the news that her shop had been broken into. "No wonder they looked at us so strangely! You have your shirt on backwards!"

Devin looked down at himself, then back at her, starting to laugh as well. "Look who's talking! Your blouse is not only inside out, but you've buttoned it up crooked."

They straightened out their clothing, then talked to the very apologetic pair of officers outside. They wanted Bonnie to meet them at the shop to take a quick look around and answer a few questions. She told them she would be there shortly, then said goodbye—a bit red in the face herself.

As Devin drove her to the shop Bonnie snuggled close to his side. "Next time," she said sagely, "we have dinner at *your* house. I'm beginning to think mine's bad luck."

CHAPTER SIX

Sunday Devin had to make an unexpected trip to Denver and would be gone overnight. Bonnie spent her day at home, practicing magic and reading. It was Monday morning before she could even bear thinking about the mess the thieves had made of her shop. Once there, she still couldn't seem to get herself motivated to begin cleaning up.

Stepping over broken jars and piles of coffee beans, her shoes making ominous crunching noises as she made her way across the floor, Marcie looked around the shop with horrified dismay. "Good grief! What in heaven's name happened?"

Bonnie was leaning on the counter with her elbows, her chin in her hands, as she looked forlornly at the herb-and-tea-strewn floor. "New merchandising scheme. You just grab a bag and sweep what you need off the floor. Like it?" she asked dejectedly.

Gingerly crossing the room on a fragrant carpet of mixed spices, Marcie joined her at the counter. "I leave for six days and you turn the place into one giant tea bag," she joked, seeing that Bonnie's spirits needed lifting.

"I'm supposed to consider myself lucky," Bonnie replied, smiling in spite of herself. "They robbed the goldsmith and splattered paint all over the artist's studio. The police think they were looking for cash hidden in my jars. I think I'll start keeping some in one labeled Money so they'll leave the rest alone next time."

"Next time?"

"Well, maybe there won't be a next time. The rest of the shop owners and I are pitching in to buy a good alarm system." She looked at Marcie, forgetting her troubles for a moment. "What are you doing here?"

Marcie gave her a sheepish grin. "You wouldn't happen to have any job openings, would you?"

"Oh, Marcie! What happened?" she asked, concerned. "I thought you had the job sewn up?"

"I did, I do. I mean, I have the job if I want it, but I don't. The owners wanted me to become a full partner, which sounded like a great opportunity till I found out they wanted me for my last name, not my brain."

"Delgado?"

Marcie nodded. "A woman *and* a Hispanic. They felt it would give them easy access to minority funding, I suppose."

"I'm so sorry."

"I'm not." And indeed, Bonnie noted, Marcie didn't look at all disappointed. "I decided I like Colorado Springs better. All my interests are here, I have good instructors at school. Not to mention boyfriends," she added with a grin. "So, what do you say? You know I'm going to keep trying, but could you use one slightly restless employee?"

Bonnie frowned, but her face brightened quickly. "I hired Megan Warner in your absence, but—"

"Oh, well, then . . ." Now Marcie did look disappointed.

"Let me finish! I think it would be a good idea to keep you both on the payroll. It's going to be a busy summer, and I could use the extra time off." The way things were going between Devin and her lately, perhaps she would need *lots* of time off! "Plus I'll have someone trained and ready should you take off on me again."

"Hey!"

"Just kidding. Besides, something else has just occurred to me," she added, a distant look in her eyes.

"Uh-oh."

"What's that supposed to mean?" Bonnie asked indignantly.

"You've got that I'm-about-to-do-something-I-shouldn't look on your face again." Marcie chuckled at Bonnie's expression of wide-eyed innocence. "How did Devin take your hiring Megan in the first place?"

"He was a bit leery, but we've gotten all that straightened out. What I'm thinking is that I may have another job for Megan," Bonnie explained. "I've been wanting to add a couple of larger illusions to my act, and I'll need some help building them and so on. She'd probably find it interesting, and it would give you more hours here."

"I appreciate that."

"I don't see why it should bother Devin," she added, unable to restrain a mischievous grin. It shouldn't bother him, but it probably would. She was coming to enjoy arguing with Devin, mainly because of the delightful ways they were finding to make up afterwards.

"From what you've told me of his protective streak, I think I'd inform him first anyway," Marcie replied skeptically.

"Maybe." Bonnie looked around the shop with dismay. "Meanwhile, I think someone should start minding the store."

Taking the broad hint, Marcie put on an apron and grabbed a broom. "Speaking of minding the store, and of things one should or shouldn't do, you didn't touch the books while I was gone, did you?"

"Well . . ."

"Uh-oh."

Devin had intended to return from Denver in the morning, but as he was leaving the local hospital his car promptly broke down. He had it towed to a nearby repair shop, where he now stood in the noisy waiting room putting a call through to Bonnie to break their lunch date.

"Bonnie?" he said, pressing the receiver against one ear and his hand against the other.

"Devin?" She could barely hear him over the awful racket in the background. "If that's what it sounds like in the hospital where you are, I think I'd rather stay sick."

"Very interesting operation taking place here," he replied, almost yelling to make himself heard. "They're pulling all sorts of parts out of this poor patient."

"Good Lord!" Bonnie exclaimed, horrified.

"No, I'm at a car hospital, not a people hospital. My car broke down again, and I'm waiting for the verdict. I hope it doesn't survive. There's a wrecking yard about a block down the road. I'm thinking of having the damn thing made into a coffee table."

"I take it this means you won't be back in time for lunch."

"You don't sound heartbroken." Devin now had to yell to be heard.

"Actually, I'm in the middle of a . . . a practice session myself," she said, turning to smile at Megan.

Megan gave Bonnie an exasperated smile, then returned to her manipulations of the silver dollar she held in her hand. "Damn, this is frustrating!" she muttered.

Over whatever noisy operation was taking place at the service station, Bonnie heard Devin's voice again, but just barely: "In other words I'm stuck here and you're busy, right? Even when our timing is perfect, it has to be in the wrong direction."

Bonnie thought of Marcie's cautionary advice and decided she had better tell Devin her plans concerning his daughter. Surely, though, he wouldn't mind if Megan helped her construct and paint a few pieces of apparatus. "Devin? I want to tell you this right away so you won't think I'm sneaking behind your back again." She hesitated for a moment. "Megan and I are going to be working closely for a while, getting some old magic equipment of mine into shape. Do you mind?"

The noise from the garage was getting louder.

"What? Oh, never mind. You can tell me tonight at dinner. My place this time, okay?"

Oh, well, Bonnie thought, at least I tried. "Sounds fine."

"What? Listen, I can't hear you, so I'll just assume you said yes. See you tonight."

Megan looked at Bonnie when she had hung up the phone. "Did you tell him about me helping you with your equipment?"

"I tried, but he was at a service station having his car worked on, and couldn't hear me."

"Honestly," Megan said, laughing affectionately, "he could drive any car he wants, but he insists on pushing that poor old thing till it dies. Even my car is newer than his."

Bonnie grinned. "There's a streak of masochism in us all when it comes to our transportation."

A customer came in, and Megan waited on him before returning to her not entirely unsuccessful attempts to make the silver dollar disappear. Bonnie watched distractedly. Megan was more dexterous than Marcie—probably something to do with the fact that her father was a surgeon. She was not, however, any more patient.

As Bonnie watched, memories rushed into her mind —memories overpowering in their clarity. A young girl, standing in front of her father, a silver dollar in her outstretched hand. "Watch this!" the girl said, excitement in her lovely green eyes. She put her hands together, then held them both out toward the man with the serious expression. He tapped her left hand. She smiled, opening it to reveal an empty palm. With a

knowing grin he tapped the other, his eyebrows shoot-
ing up when her other hand was empty as well. When
she reached into his coat pocket and brought out the
silver dollar, he laughed and laughed, a fierce pride
burning inside him when she asked, "Will you teach
me more?"

Slowly coming back to the here and now, Bonnie
realized Megan was standing in front of her, waiting
expectantly for an answer to the very same question
she had just heard in her thoughts. "I'm sorry, I was
daydreaming. I'd be glad to teach you more. What
would you like to learn?"

"Well, the sleight of hand is fun, I suppose, but it's
so . . . so technical," Megan replied. She gave Bonnie a sly wink. "I was wondering if you could teach me
some *real* magic."

An alarm went off in Bonnie's head. "Real magic?"

"Yes. *You* know," she added, as if Bonnie surely had
to understand.

"I'm not sure I follow you."

"Psychic abilities, mind reading, that sort of thing,"
Megan explained, a confused look on her face.

"Spiritualism?" Bonnie asked nonchalantly.

Megan's expression and voice suddenly turned cau-
tious. "I suppose."

Pursing her lips, Bonnie took Megan's hand. "Come
on. Let's go to lunch. I think it's time you and I had a
serious talk."

Over the restaurant's special chicken-fried steak,
Bonnie proceeded to try to unravel Megan's desire for
such knowledge, finding it an arduous task indeed.

All she really succeeded in doing was to put Megan

on the defensive. "So you're saying you don't believe in psychic phenomena?"

"As I was telling you," Bonnie said patiently, "ninety-nine percent of the time there's magic—illusion—involved."

"And the remaining one percent?" Megan asked, bright-eyed.

Bonnie sighed in exasperation. "I'll tell you what I told Devin. I've seen things that would stand your hair on end. And, unlike your father, I believe there are some pretty strange and wonderful things going on in the world around us, things not only unexplained but unexplainable." Megan nodded, obviously intrigued—something Bonnie did not fail to observe. "But I'm a skeptic, it comes with the profession of magic. As you become more and more skilled, you also become more adept at separating reality from illusion."

"I see," Megan replied with an air of disenchantment.

But Bonnie didn't think she saw at all. Her young employee seemed disturbed by her words and was unusually uncommunicative for the rest of the day. When she took off for another of her mysterious appointments that evening, Bonnie couldn't miss the anxiety on her face, and couldn't shake the feeling that it was caused by their lunchtime discussion. Whether inspired by otherworldly sources or not, Bonnie felt confident in making a prediction: Megan was in for more of an education than she had bargained for.

This was it. Bonnie could feel it in her bones. The night ahead fairly glistened with the promise of passion, a mutual passion Devin and she had shared all too briefly before. This time nothing would stand in the way of their full enjoyment of each other, nothing would interrupt the beautiful afterglow. This night was theirs completely, without ringing phones or well-meaning policemen. At the risk of tempting fate, she simply couldn't imagine anything else that could possibly go wrong.

When he had called just minutes earlier, to tell her he had gotten back safely and to make sure she had heard his invitation, her pulse had started singing in high gear. He wasn't on call, Marcie was back in town and could handle any surprises with the shop, and Devin had assured her that his phones would be unplugged the whole evening. The whole evening! A delicious anticipation swelled within her at the mere thought of Devin and their plans for this night, plans that she knew were identical. If this was obsession, then it was very sweet indeed.

After parking her car alongside Devin's—noticing with amusement the new, foot-shaped dent in the fender—she hurried to the front door, her coat flung over one arm.

"Bonnie, come in," Devin greeted, opening the door before she had a chance to knock.

His eyes devoured her as she stepped into the living room. She wore a low-cut dress, a brilliant multicolored silk gown that skimmed her figure, the hem, in a dipping handkerchief style, ending just below her knees. Her hair was loose, the way he preferred it, but held back on both sides by shining combs of intricately carved mother-of-pearl.

118

"Breathtaking," he murmured, taking her coat.

"Thank you," she replied, for some reason a bit unsure of herself all of a sudden. Then she gave herself a mental shove. She wanted him, and he wanted her. There was nothing wrong with wanting more of the delicious tenderness they had already shared. "Devin," she whispered, her hands reaching up to touch him. She felt an immediacy, an unwillingness to give anything a chance to stop the marvelous feeling of being close to him. Sliding her arms around his neck, she drew him closer, her coat falling to the floor forgotten.

Devin, too, seemed to feel an urgency, and he communicated it to her as his arms enclosed her in a tight embrace. "I know we have all night, but somehow I feel . . ." His voice trailed off as he buried his face in her hair and inhaled deeply, the scent of the exotic drifting into his senses as if diffused by some passion-inducing flower. He could feel her firm breasts pressing against his chest, her thighs tight against his own. She ran her fingers through his hair, relishing its smoothness.

"If you're trying to say you think we should skip right to dessert," she said, her voice a whisper, "I wouldn't mind." She moved back, only slightly, enough to give her fingers room to caress his firm neck, stroke his broad shoulders. Then with one hand she started to unbutton his shirt, and with the other she explored the warm skin she had uncovered, stopping as she heard his sharp intake of breath when she reached his belt.

"You *are* dessert, sweet Bonnie, and I've always enjoyed my desserts first." Devin gasped again as Bonnie ran her nails up and down his hair-strewn chest, slipping a bit farther inside his jeans with each downward movement. He was dressed casually tonight, but only because he hadn't intended to stay dressed for very long anyway. Realizing he would soon be unable to stand at all if she continued her sweet torture, he abruptly swung her into his arms.

"You have too much on," he declared, striding quickly up the stairs to his bedroom.

"I think that can be remedied."

"You bet it can!" He kicked the door open in front of them. "It's a good thing you're such a lightweight," he teased.

"Lightweight?" she questioned haughtily.

"Only in terms of actual weight, I assure you."

"Are you implying, sir, that you couldn't carry me around if I weighed any more? If so, then I would say *you* are the lightweight." Her voice teased him back, her teeth nipping at his earlobe.

Swinging her around the room in playful outrage, he asked defiantly, "Are you impugning my masculinity?"

"I told you I'd get back at you for impugning my profession."

Devin set her on the bed unceremoniously. "At any rate, you're talking about muscle, not masculinity. There is a difference, you know, you female chauvinist." Devin's eyes smoldered with a desire just barely held in check. "You're about to find out all about my masculinity," he said, the murmured words an infinite promise. Quick fingers unzipped her dress, their movements no less quick as one by one all her remaining garments followed it to the floor. Stripping off his own clothes, he joined her on the bed, seeking her softness and warmth. "Hey, where are you going?"

"Just making room for you," she replied, sliding to the center of the bed, her hair a trail of fire across the whiteness of the sheets.

"Such beautiful hair." Devin softly stroked the silky tendrils, his lips running kisses up her delicate arms as they stretched out to him in welcome. "You're a feast for the senses. Fiery hair, soft pink-and-white skin," he murmured, nuzzling her nape.

Bonnie reached out to touch him, wanting to feel his warmth against her, to have the raging fire inside her unite with his and surround them both in flames. His lips moved gently over hers at first, then the urgency of his desire overwhelmed him, demanding, consuming, drawing her deeper. She stroked his feverish skin wanting to touch all of him at once. Soft kisses rained over her face, but again and again his mouth returned to hers, thirsty and possessive.

Moaning softly, Bonnie arched her sleek form against his hardness when his head dipped to touch her swollen breasts with a flickering tongue. She felt as though she were melting as he suckled first one, then the other, a startled, delighted gasp escaping from her throat at the delicate nip of his teeth.

A shrill wail broke the silence of the night. They both sat bolt upright on the bed.

"What's that!" Bonnie cried, holding her hands over her ears to block out the unearthly clamor.

"Oh, my God!" Devin yelled, his expression a mixture of anger and alarm. He leapt off the bed, going to the bedroom door.

"What's wrong?" she asked in a startled voice.

Perturbed now, he grabbed his robe and opened the door, sniffing the air. "That blasted smoke alarm," he said as he left the room to head for the kitchen. Bonnie could hear him grumble as he went down the stairs: "I knew I should have bought the more expensive model."

Bonnie collapsed back on the bed, breathing a sigh of relief when the shrill sound stopped. "And I thought nothing else could go wrong," she muttered in exasperation. She felt like stomping her feet or pounding the pillows with her fists. Frustration, she decided, was very bad for the body.

Then a whiff of smoke reached her. Maybe it wasn't a false alarm after all! Springing to her feet, she grabbed Devin's shirt, putting it on as she followed the sound of his cursing voice. The smell of smoke grew stronger as she got closer to the kitchen.

When she opened the door, she found the kitchen full of smoke. It hit her immediately, causing tears to well in her eyes. In the middle of the choking cloud stood a very angry man swearing mightily as he flipped the exhaust fan over the stove to high.

"What—what can I do to help?" Bonnie choked the words out.

"Poof! Make it all go away like magic," he teased through a coughing fit of his own.

"Careful," she threatened playfully. "You're already close to disappearing in a puff of smoke! Are you all right?"

"Just fine. Close that door, will you? No use spreading smoke all over the house." He opened all the kitchen windows, and the back door, then went to the adjoining garage.

He returned with a large fan, which he set on a table near a window. As the fan pulled the smoke from the room, the air cleared quickly. When Bonnie opened the oven door, however, a fresh stream of smoke assailed them. Grabbing a pot holder, she removed the culprit from inside. "What is—or should I say was—this?" she asked, gingerly tossing the smoldering remnant into the sink and dousing it with water.

"A gourmet frozen entrée."

"This is what I was getting for dinner?" she asked in forlorn amusement.

"No. That's from another night," Devin answered distractedly as he moved the fan for the best effect.

"You've been cooking it all this time?" She looked at the soggy black lump in the sink.

Glancing at her, he did a double take and looked directly at her for the first time through the clearing air. She was wearing his shirt—just his shirt. The tails ended mid thigh and revealed much more than they concealed. Only two buttons were done up, giving him a tantalizing view of her smooth shoulders and her creamy breasts, their pink tips hard against the soft cotton material. The sight of her slim legs was no less enticing, which made him keenly aware of the heat still burning strongly within him.

"Devin?" she murmured, alive to the sensuality of his gaze.

"Hmm? Oh. That thing in the sink was supposed to

have been my dinner a few nights ago, but I got called away. I just turned the oven off and forgot about it."

"I think it's done."

"Well done, I'd say," he replied, smiling at her. "I was going to broil some chicken breasts for us tonight and had just turned on the oven when you drove up. After I opened the door," he continued, his eyes roving over her, "I forgot everything. Everything but you."

Smiling back at him, she shook her head in wonder. Were they ever going to get the chance to simply lie in each other's arms, enjoying the sweet exhaustion of their desire?

The air was clear now, and Devin hurriedly turned off the fan, closed the windows, and locked the back door before moving purposefully toward her. She watched the lean and tautly muscled figure in the loosely tied robe that left his manhood free from doubt. "I declare this emergency over," Bonnie stated quietly.

"And I declare another just beginning." Pulling her into his arms, he hugged her close. "Could I impose upon you to show me just where we left off?" he whispered.

"My pleasure. Just follow me," she answered seductively.

"Anywhere, anytime," he returned, enjoying the sight of her as he followed her up the stairs.

The sound of a very loud and very big truck pulling into the driveway halted their progress. Flashing red lights flickered across the curtains below them.

"No, no, no!" Bonnie moaned as a demanding knock sounded on the front door.

"Go on upstairs," Devin said with a deep sigh, wrapping his robe tighter around his hips. "And remember my place."

From the bedroom Bonnie could hear Devin explaining all the smoke to a fireman with a good sense of humor. Next she heard the truck back noisily out of the driveway, then Devin's footsteps on the stairs.

"A concerned neighbor called the fire department," he explained, hastily removing his robe. "Now, where were we?" he asked, unbuttoning the two buttons and easing the shirt from Bonnie's shoulders.

"Mmm. Right there will do fine," she replied with a moan as his teeth gently nipped at the sensitive skin of her throat.

Another knock sounded from below, quickly accompanied by the sound of a key in the lock and an apologetic voice calling from the foot of the stairs: "Dad? It's Megan. The hospital's been trying to track you down."

Devin swung his legs to the floor and sat on the edge of the bed, his face in his hands. "Ever seen a grown man cry?" he asked, the exasperation in his voice tempered with the dry humor Bonnie had come to love.

"You'd better go find out what they want," Bonnie said, wondering where on earth she was getting the patience and understanding she felt.

Quiet voices drifted up to her as Devin talked, first to Megan, then to someone on the phone. When he returned, he walked directly to the closet and dropped

125

his robe. "I have to go. Trouble with a cornea transplant," he said, then proceeded to dress in frustrated silence.

"Devin . . ." Bonnie began, wanting to reassure him, ease away the worried look so apparent on his face—a look she knew had nothing to do with whatever was wrong at the hospital.

"I have to go, this can't wait. Damn it! I'm so sorry, Bonnie."

"Devin, go. I understand." She really *did* understand. Although, in all honesty, she wanted him here with her, she knew he wouldn't be the man he was without his work, his dedication. He wouldn't be the man she loved.

"I'll most likely be gone all night. I'll call you tomorrow," he promised, pulling her into his arms, savoring the feel and scent of her, allowing himself one quick kiss before releasing her.

"I'll lock up here and make sure everything's okay. You go perform some magic," she teased with a warm smile.

Taking one last lingering look at her lying there among the bed sheets, he sighed loudly. "Thank you. Are you sure you'll be okay?"

"I'll be fine. I think I'll call my mother."

"To tell her about the horrible man who walks out on you all the time?" he asked.

"You're wonderful. I'm going to ask her if she knows how to break a curse. I think someone's put one on our love life," she quipped, enjoying the broad grin he gave her from the doorway.

"Good idea." He had to be insane, he thought, to

walk out on a beautiful woman like Bonnie. But he had to do it, and he knew it. He also knew she wasn't lying when she said she understood, and somehow that made her all the more beautiful. "Talk to you tomorrow." Devin left quickly before he gave in to the temptation lying there.

Not knowing whether to laugh or cry, Bonnie dressed and checked the house over before going home to make and eat a lonely dinner. Lying in an equally lonely bed, she had a dismal thought: Would one night be all Devin and she had? One night of soaring delight, and even that interrupted at the point where other delicious emotions besides desire were entering the picture for them? No! For her at least, even with the interruptions, a step forward had been taken in their relationship tonight. Bonnie realized she loved Devin.

And then another startling realization struck her: This was the man. *The* man. She wanted him, wanted to bed Devin Warner as often as she could, and wed him as soon as she could. I hope he feels the same way, she thought. He had better! Nobody messes with a sorcerer! And with a devilish smile on her face she slowly drifted off to sleep.

CHAPTER SEVEN

The night was cool and crisp, the air scrubbed clean by the rain that had fallen all day. Even now a misty drizzle continued. And somewhere up above, Bonnie knew, the gray clouds concealed the full moon whose filtered light bathed her in a hazy glow. It was a perfect night for playing detective. All I need now is some lightning, she thought as she sat in her car watching the front door of a plain ranch-style house on the north side of town.

As if on cue, the sky lit up with a flash. "Terrific," she muttered. "Now where's Vincent Price?" Stretching to ease her stiff legs, Bonnie settled herself—and her imagination—down to continue surveillance of the house Megan had disappeared into a half hour earlier. Again she felt a pang of guilt for having followed Megan on one of her appointments, but she quickly pushed it aside. She was doing this as much to help Megan as to satisfy her own admittedly enormous curiosity.

Truth to tell, she had resorted to stealth only because neither Devin nor his daughter seemed inclined to talk about their mutual secret, a secret Bonnie had the uneasy feeling could eventually get in the way of her growing love for him. She *had* to know what was going on, and since nobody was climbing over himself to tell her, she would find out for herself.

Actually, she had already discovered enough to put her mind at ease, at least partially so. After waiting for Megan to go inside, Bonnie had parked in the shadows of an elm at the opposite side of the quiet street. Her headlights had illuminated a discreet sign on the lawn: Madame Trisha, Adviser. If Devin knew about Megan's evening escapades, it was no wonder that he had been worried about her meeting Bonnie, before he himself had had a chance to discover more about the Mysterious Tyson.

At last Megan came out, walking toward her car with what Bonnie decided was a rather dejected gait. Stepping out of her own car and into the light of a street lamp, Bonnie waited until she was sure Megan saw her, then she spoke:

"Hello, Megan."

Megan stopped in her tracks, looking not so much startled as guilty. "Bonnie, I—you followed me," she said accusingly.

Bonnie imagined there was some guilt displayed on her own face as well. "I'm sorry, but yes, I did follow you. I was worried about you." She waved her hand in the direction of Madame Trisha's residence. "I still am."

Closing the distance between them, Megan looked at her seriously. "Did Dad send you?"

"No. He thinks I'm doing a benefit show at the Elks' lodge. He doesn't even know I suspected this was the cause of the tension between you two, and that's something I plan to discuss with him later. Right now I think it's time you told me what's going on." It's time *somebody* did, she thought dismally.

"Why should I?" Megan asked defiantly. "You're no more a believer than he is."

"Because you're my friend," Bonnie replied gently. "And you know my mind is much more open than Devin's. Why didn't you confide in me?" It was a question she planned to ask Devin as well.

Megan's defiance deflated like a punctured balloon, and tears welled in her blue eyes. "Because you and Dad were getting so close, and I didn't want him to know. He thinks I've given up going to mediums. Then, at lunch, you sounded so skeptical and I—Oh, Bonnie!" she sobbed, tears rolling down her cheeks.

Putting an arm around her shoulders, Bonnie led Megan to her car. "Let's go to my place, have some hot tea, and talk. Okay?"

"I'd like that very much."

"Can you drive?" Bonnie asked as Megan slipped beneath the wheel. Megan smiled and nodded.

At Bonnie's house they sat at the kitchen table and continued their discussion. "Madame Trisha is the seventh clairvoyant I've consulted in the last three years," Megan was saying. "I'm trying to find my mother. Dad didn't tell you?" she asked hesitantly.

"No." Bonnie felt a disjointed anger boiling within her. Part of that anger was directed at the opportunistic people Megan had chosen to place her all-too-willing trust in. But a very healthy portion was now directed at Devin as well. "No, he didn't."

130

"Oh." Megan looked confused. "Then maybe I shouldn't—"

"I intend to talk with your father later. I'll get the whole story from him, I assure you." And you'd better believe it, Bonnie thought. Even if she had to strangle him first. Come to think of it, strangling him would not be such a bad idea in any case. "Right now I'm worried about you. I take it your mother's alive?"

"We don't know," Megan said dejectedly. "She dropped out of sight."

"And these . . ." Bonnie, struggling to control her irritation, had to clear her throat before she could continue. "These people you've consulted. Have they helped?"

"No."

"Do you believe they can?"

"Oh, Bonnie, I don't know what to believe anymore. The first one I went to, not long after I turned eighteen—well, I should have learned my lesson," she said with a sigh, her elbows propped on the table and her chin in her hands. "It was like pouring money down a hole in the ground. Dad absolutely exploded when he found out. I suppose I blamed him when ordinary methods failed to turn up any sign of my mother, and I know I continued trying medium after medium from then on as much to spite him as anything. He was so negative, you know?"

Bonnie smiled wryly in spite of herself. "Yes, I know."

"Anyway, I got over blaming him for anything, and he got over blowing up at me, but I continued to try and it's caused a lot of tension between us."

131

"He's just worried about you, Megan," Bonnie said softly.

"I know. He's been so patient with me. I think he finally understood that I felt I had to do something, that it made me happy just to be trying. And it did too. Up until our talk yesterday."

With a deep sigh Bonnie poured them both another cup of tea from a kettle on the stove, then returned to her seat, looking at Megan apologetically. "I didn't mean to take your hopes away, Megan. Devin hadn't told me anything, and you were so secretive as well. It's a habit of mine to poke and prod something I don't understand, until either I figure it out or it falls apart. I'm sorry."

"Don't be," Megan said warmly. "You haven't taken away my hope, you only made me realize I've been fooling myself all this time. I'm as much of a skeptic as you are. These people I thought could help were preying on my weakness, and deep down I knew it. I don't know why, but I blinded myself to the facts. I've been such a fool," she finished miserably.

"You were hurting and looking for any way to make the hurting stop. Don't be so hard on yourself," Bonnie scolded softly. "Have you ever read about Harry Houdini?"

"Hah! How does that help? I know he debunked the claims of hundreds of charlatan clairvoyants and spiritualists. Knowing that, you would have thought I'd have more sense than to keep going to them."

"Ah, but remember this: Houdini was so hard on fake mediums because he was looking for a real one, one who could actually perform as claimed. He was interested in spiritualism because he wanted to speak with his mother, who had died some years earlier."

"But he never found one."

"No. And I've never seen a flying saucer, but that doesn't mean they don't exist. An open mind with a healthy dose of skepticism served Houdini well, and I think we can all learn from that philosophy."

Megan laughed. "I suppose you're right. At least it's more interesting than going around disbelieving everything."

"Now you've got the idea," Bonnie replied, laughing too.

"Thanks, Bonnie."

"What are friends for? Now, you look dragged out. Go home and get some rest, and we'll talk some more tomorrow. Meanwhile I have some unfinished business."

"Dad?"

Bonnie nodded. "We need to have a little talk too. I have serious doubts, however, that it will be nearly as calm and quiet as ours just was."

Bonnie was pleased with the happy, relieved look on Megan's face as she escorted the younger woman to the door. She was glad she had gotten to the bottom of this, glad she had been able to help, and hoped to help even more. But a slow-boiling anger still bubbled within her. Devin hadn't seen fit to take her into his confidence despite their growing intimacy, and that hurt. She loved him, but she had to know where she stood.

There were a lot of unanswered questions about Megan's mother, questions Bonnie could kick herself for not having asked earlier—before she had lost her heart to Devin. Whether the answers would be painful, for Devin or her, didn't matter much to her anymore. Nothing could be as painful as knowing Devin hadn't trusted her enough to supply them without being asked.

"Bonnie!" Devin exclaimed when he opened his door to find her standing there.

Not waiting for an invitation, Bonnie strode past him to the living room before turning on her heel to confront him. She was dressed for business, in blue jeans and a white cotton turtleneck. It appealed to her sense of the dramatic to be able to push the long sleeves up to her elbows as she glared at him. "We have a thing or two to discuss, you and I," she began.

Devin's eyebrows arched. "Shall I get the boxing gloves?"

"It may well come to that," she said, her temper escalating as she noted his amused expression. "First I want you as mad as I am."

"What's this all about?" he asked, looking at her as if she had lost her mind. "I thought you were working tonight."

"That'll do for starters. I lied."

"You—Why? Bonnie, you knew I had the night off, that I wasn't on call. We could have . . ."

His eyes had narrowed slightly, but she could tell he was mildly perturbed, not angry. She didn't want to yell at him if he wasn't going to yell back, and she felt decidedly like yelling. "Not enough, huh? Okay. Instead of being here, with you, I was out sneaking behind your back again," Bonnie said vindictively, "following your daughter!"

Devin's eyes widened, and his face began to redden. "Following her! What on earth for?" he exclaimed, his confusion tinged with anger.

Hands on hips, Bonnie leaned forward as she spoke, allowing her rage to carry her away. "Because I'd had enough of your damned secrets, that's why! It was obvious you weren't going to tell me anything, so I had to go looking for my own answers."

"I don't know what you're talking about," Devin replied, dismissing her argument with a wave of his hand.

"Then how's this, Mr. Innocent? Tonight, while you thought I was working, I followed Megan to the medium she's been seeing for the past week," Bonnie announced in furious triumph. "Are you still going to tell me you haven't been keeping things from me?"

Suddenly Devin lost the hold he had on his temper. "What!" he yelled.

Yes, she thought, there it was. Color in his face, snap to his voice. A good, loud, angry yell. Now they could get on with this discussion. "Why didn't you tell me?" she yelled back. "Why did you make me go looking for answers about your past?" Devin opened his mouth to speak, but she wasn't finished yet. "And, Devin, if you say you didn't tell me because I didn't ask, so help me . . ." she fumed.

"Damn that's infuriating!" he burst out. "If you like a good argument so much, I'll give you one, but let me hold up my half without speaking it for me!"

"All right!" Bonnie shot back.

"Good!" Devin replied, just as loudly.

"Well?" she demanded.

"Well, what?"

Bonnie clenched her fists in exasperation. She was at the point of losing control completely, of allowing her inflamed temper to carry her beyond reason toward heaven knew what reaction. She couldn't remember being this angry with anyone ever before. "Why didn't you tell me?" She ground out the words between clenched teeth.

"Why didn't you ask?" Devin said tauntingly.

Her control snapped. So infuriated she didn't know what came over her, Bonnie tried to get Devin in a judo hold she had learned some years ago in Japan, intending to throw him onto the couch.

But Devin obviously knew more than she did, and held his ground, letting her struggle for a moment before reversing the hold and tossing her casually to the couch instead. "Hah!" he exclaimed triumphantly.

"Damn you," Bonnie muttered, nothing hurt but her pride. "I should have asked. I thought it might be painful for you—thought you'd tell me about Megan's mother when we got to know each other better," she added miserably.

Devin sat down on the couch beside her, sighing audibly. "And I should have told you. It is painful for me, but I should have told you."

Bonnie was huffing and puffing from her exertions. Devin's calm breathing irritated her. "The least you could do is breathe hard!" she fumed.

Pulling her hip tightly against his, he winked slyly at her. "That can be arranged."

"You're insufferable." She sniffed.

"Never said I wasn't," he agreed amiably.

Her breathing almost back to normal, Bonnie looked at him seriously. "I'm asking. Are you telling?"

Devin released her and leaned back on the couch, running his hands over his face before returning her intent gaze. "It happened in my second year of college. I was seventeen, and—"

"Whoa! A sophomore at seventeen?"

Devin grinned wryly. "Yeah. I was precociously intelligent, or so they told me. I was bright, I suppose, but I was still a snotty-nosed kid. Had all the common sense of your average brick wall."

Devin seemed to retreat into his memories. His face had held amusement before, but now his expression turned serious.

"Go on," Bonnie urged gently.

"Her name was Daphne. We weren't in love. Didn't even like each other all that much really. But I was young, inexperienced, and painfully eager. She was— oh, hell, I don't know what she was. She was there, and willing. God . . ." His voice broke with the strength of the memory.

"Devin," Bonnie whispered compassionately. "We've all done things we could kick ourselves for, especially when we were young. Some of them we can laugh about later, and some will pain us till the end of our days. It's only human."

"I know," he said with a heavy sigh. "I know. I have such ambiguous feelings about that night. I barely remember it at all, except for my incredible

137

naïveté, and yet it turned out to be the most important night of my life. How can I regret the night Megan was conceived? How can I regret having participated in bringing such a delightful young woman into the world?"

"She's very special," Bonnie agreed.

"To me she is," Devin said fiercely. "But to Daphne —" He broke off again but slowly brought himself under control. "Neither of us wanted to marry, but I insisted all the same. It wasn't the same being a single parent twenty years ago as it is now, and there weren't as many options. She hated being married, hated me for making her carry our child to full term." A tear trickled down Devin's cheek. Several moments passed before he could continue, but Bonnie said nothing, knowing there was nothing she could say. He spoke again at last, his voice rough with emotion: "After Megan was born, Daphne's disposition got even worse. She wanted freedom. Fun. I tried, I really tried, but there was no reasoning with her. Megan was barely a year old when she left."

Now Bonnie had to speak. "My God! She just left?"

Devin nodded. "Luckily, for me and for Megan, my parents stepped in at that point. I didn't know what I was going to do. I would have had to quit school, get a job. I would have had to leave Megan with a baby-sitter during the most important years of her life. But they took us in, saw to it that I stayed in school and that Megan had a loving, supportive home. My mother gave her all the love and attention Daphne had denied her, and she really had two doting fathers—my dad and myself." Devin finally smiled again, and Bonnie smiled with him. "I spent as much time with her as I could. More, I suppose, than I would have otherwise."

Bonnie was crying unabashedly. "She's turned into a wonderful young woman, Devin. My mother used to tell me that things have a way of working out for the best, no matter how hard you try to stop them. Megan flourished, and you became the caring physician you were meant to be. You shouldn't feel guilty at all."

Devin turned to her and clasped her tightly in his arms. "She is wonderful, isn't she? Now you see why I'm so protective of her, why I get so upset with her as well. Why does she insist on finding her mother? As far as I'm concerned, Daphne's dead. She left us, dropped completely out of sight. She didn't even surface when I filed for the divorce." His expression turned hard and forbidding. "Why can't Megan leave well enough alone?"

Divorced. A flood of relief washed over Bonnie. Confused by his sudden anxiety, however, she could only explain what she imagined Megan's feelings were. "Daphne is Megan's birth-mother. Besides a natural curiosity, Megan's bound to feel a certain need to find her, to meet a missing part of her past face to face, so to speak. She's as strong-minded as you are, Devin. There's no stopping her from trying."

Devin sighed heavily. "I know. I've known it for some time, I guess. I suppose there's no harm in her trying, is there?"

Bonnie smiled at the questioning tone in his voice. "I suppose not, though she's just spinning her wheels at the moment. I set her straight on a few things to-

139

night, and we'll have a long talk tomorrow. I have a few ideas of my own," she said enigmatically. "We've become friends. I've more than a passing interest in her well-being."

There was a worried expression on Devin's face as she spoke, but it faded quickly. There was a closeness between them now that they could both feel in their bones. In her own way Bonnie was every bit as protective of Megan as Devin was. It gave them a common ground, a tender understanding.

"Do you realize," Devin said, his voice a low murmur, "that there is absolutely nothing to stop me from making love to you tonight?"

"Nothing?" she asked, running one finger along his collar.

"I'm not on call. I've finally hired an answering service to screen out everything but the most dire emergencies—most of which my partners will now handle. Nothing's in the oven, and I assume you alerted someone to the fact that you wouldn't be available for a while, at least not until you had finished playing Sam Spade with my daughter?"

"I see our minds have been working along similar lines. I have that call-forwarding service on my phone as of today," Bonnie replied as she began unbuttoning his shirt. "Marcie's job in Fort Collins fell through, so she's back working for me and has all my calls till tomorrow morning. Even the salesmen."

"Low sales resistance?"

"To you, definitely," she said, then smiled at him mischievously. "Actually, I'm still supposed to be mad at you. That could be one thing standing in your way."

"So take your anger out on my body," he replied, blue eyes twinkling.

"Sounds promising." She ran her nails down his now-uncovered chest, appreciating his sharp intake of breath. "Mmm. It *is* promising, isn't it?"

Devin ran his hands underneath her shirt, warm fingers caressing her smooth midriff. "Very." Sliding his hands up, he cupped her full breasts, kneading them gently.

She moaned as he slipped her turtleneck off, then unclasped her brassiere, his warm flesh now encircling hers. Smooth thumb pads moved back and forth across her nipples, bringing them to a taut erectness, the ache inside her all at once foremost in her mind. She leaned her head on his shoulder and gave in to the passions consuming her. "Oh, yes," she whispered, arching her body against his hands, her fingers digging into his thighs as he stroked her trembling form.

Devin slipped his hands into the front pockets of her jeans, holding her captive while he plunged his tongue into her waiting mouth. One wandering finger ventured deep into her pocket, caressing, teasing, searching until she cried out in surprise and desire. "Devin!"

"Yes?" he murmured, slowly unzipping her jeans.

"I . . . I want . . ."

"Your wish is my command," he returned huskily. Strong arms swept her up, holding her against his warm chest. He carried her to his bedroom, laying her across the bed, then standing back to look at her in

141

wonder. Wet parted lips just begging to be kissed. Swollen breasts aching for his touch. Smooth belly encased in unzipped jeans with just a hint of white lace peeking out to taunt him.

Stepping closer, he let one finger caress her cheekbone, then let it glide over her parted lips, feeling her hot breath warm him before he cupped her chin in his hands. Her tongue darted out to tease his thumb as he tenderly touched her lips, her teeth nipping it playfully.

Bonnie couldn't take his teasing anymore. She wanted to feel his chest against hers, to feel his lips dance over all the places he had just touched and those he caressed with his smoldering gaze. She wanted to discover every muscle and line of his body, if it took her a lifetime and beyond. As she held her arms up to him in demanding invitation, her eyes spoke her desire more clearly than her soft whisper could. "Come to me."

Devin slowly backed up and removed his clothes, his eyes never leaving hers. Then he trailed one hand up her leg, following the inside seam of her jeans to the apex. As he cupped her, her soft moan made his senses jump in harmony with hers. He held still, calming himself for the slow seduction he had planned. His errant thumb wandered up to touch white lace, sliding underneath the thin elastic to brush soft curls with a feather-light caress.

Eyes shut, soft gasps flowing free, breasts heaving with every breath, Bonnie again reached out to him, but again he eluded her grasp. She arched her hips readily to help as he tugged her jeans down her slim legs. Opening her eyes, she was stunned by the magnificence of his body. His golden chest, strong arms, and lean hips and thighs waited for her touch. She moved to sit up, but he stopped her, holding one slim ankle in the palm of his hand and stroking the sensitive area behind her knee.

Devin gently bit her toes, the feeling more erotic than she could ever have imagined. "Devin," she moaned, arching her body toward him, her message obvious as he stroked her inner thighs, coming closer to the heart of her with each caress. Wet kisses and delicate teeth followed the trail his hands had blazed, not one inch left unexplored.

"Patience," he whispered. Removing the last barrier, a filmy bit of lace, his hand came to rest on her stomach. His face dropped suddenly to drink the softness of her belly, tongue drawing an exacting picture of her navel before plunging into its middle.

"Oh, please," she cried, her hands finally able to reach him. She grasped his head, her fingers running through the smooth strands of his hair, feeling sparks of excitement shoot through her.

"Stop?" he questioned throatily as his lips traveled a sure path to her waiting breasts. They were taut and ready, the nipples hard beneath his tongue.

"No!" At last his delicious weight descended upon her, his body stretching onto hers, his hardness pressing into soft, yielding flesh. Pinning her arms above her head, with his lips he sought the warm hollow of her throat and traced the delicate bones of her neck, his tongue darting out to touch a leaping point of pulse. He looked at her, a devilish smile on his face as he watched her passion-parched lips, inviting him, coaxing him closer.

"No?"

A moan of impatience escaped her, her instincts taking over to entice him to do her will. She moved beneath him, slowly, sensually, her demanding hips arching against his. It drove him wild. He plundered her mouth, punished her gently for her deviltry. Again her hips arched in feminine demand, and he gladly gave in to his own raging passion. Their bodies merged into one, both feeling the volcano of mutual desire and need shower them with a sparkling, brilliant light.

Their lovemaking was intensely, feverishly urgent. They consumed each other, demanded and received their pleasure in a rushing tumult of fire. Only then could they discover the opposite of their previous, near-violent desire, find the tender and gentle path to the same shuddering heights. Rational thought returned slowly, and they were soon covered by the soft blanket of sleep, still wrapped possessively in each other's arms.

"Is that your stomach or mine?" Bonnie asked lazily. Her head rested on his chest, their bodies touched from shoulder to toe. She felt totally relaxed for the first time in weeks.

"Must be mine," he murmured. "Even without dinner yours is too ladylike to growl in that manner." At that precise moment her stomach chose to belie his statement. They both burst out laughing as their hungry bodies talked to each other.

"What's for dinner?"

144

"I'm not sure. I suggest we move ourselves into the kitchen and find out. We'll need hearty sustenance for the night ahead," Devin replied roguishly.

"Oh?" she asked, eyes wide open and twinkling at him. "Rough water ahead?"

He kissed her on the tip of her nose. "I plan on smooth sailing all the way till dawn."

Together they raided the refrigerator, experimenting and tasting until their hunger was satisfied—at least for food. Other appetites soon entered their minds.

Bonnie could feel a slow burning warm to a roaring fire as she thought of the evening ahead. She watched as Devin restored order to the kitchen. He was clad only in low-slung jeans, his sure movements quick and precise, with no wasted steps. It was his turn now, she decided. She intended to know his body intimately by morning, to trace, touch, and taste every inch of him. There would be no escaping her.

She walked over to where he stood at the sink, and slid her arms around him, rubbing her breasts against the tanned skin of his broad back. Her body quivered at the warmth between them. "I have an idea," she whispered.

"So do I," he said with a groan. He shut off the water and turned into her softness.

"I bet I can tell you what yours is."

"Then don't tell, show," Devin invited, his body humming from the movement of her delicate hands on his waist.

"Mmm." Releasing him, she stepped away and picked up a chopstick, laughing at his startled look, then walked back to the bedroom, confident he would

145

follow. She entered the master bathroom and turned the taps on full force, then deftly piled her hair on top of her head, securing it with the chopstick.

"Oh," Devin said as he watched her from the doorway. "I thought you were going to do something kinky."

Bonnie simply smirked and shed the shirt she was wearing, before sinking into the warm water of the sunken marble tub. Her breasts seemed to peek out at him invitingly through the rising steam, though she noticed he didn't need any encouragement. "Clean, not kinky," she said, sitting up and pouring water over her shoulders. "Join me?"

He hungrily watched the rivulets run down her shoulders and breasts. "Definitely." His fingers fumbled with the buttons of his jeans in his haste, and he finally managed to kick them off. The look in her eyes caused him to stand still for a moment. Did those green eyes hold desire, lust, or something more? He wasn't sure; he only knew that for now whatever was there was enough.

She marveled in appreciation as he joined her in the tub, loving the look of his body in the full light. His well-proportioned chest and arms blended nicely with his lean waist, slim hips, and muscled thighs; his masculinity was beyond doubt.

Her open perusal of his body excited him even more. Her obvious pleasure in the sight of him warmed him even more than the hot water of the bath. He leaned back, stretched his legs out beside hers, and closed his eyes with a sigh, relaxed. But not for long.

"Bonnie!" he yelped, jerking up and sloshing water everywhere.

Mischievous delight danced in her eyes. She was resting comfortably against the other side of the large tub. One foot rose out of the water, her painted toes wiggling at him. "Very talented creatures, a magician's toes. Did you know Houdini could shuffle cards with his feet?" Moving closer she dexterously pulled the hairs on his chest.

"Hey!" He grabbed her foot and pulled her to him, anchoring her slippery form between his thighs.

"You were the one thinking kinky thoughts."

"I'm trying to relax," he replied haughtily.

She leaned closer and kissed his chest. "I'll help."

Devin leaned back again, closing his eyes as Bonnie picked up the soap and worked up a good lather before starting to wash him. Her hands explored him, stroking him clean, working her way over his arms, then down his chest to his thighs. Nice muscle development, she thought. Passing first over one sensitive area, she went on to find two others—his feet.

It was all Devin could do to sit still while she washed each foot, stroking the arches, giving attention to each toe. "Now cut that out!" he cried when he could take it no longer.

"Don't rush me. I think you have very nice feet."

"I didn't know you had a foot fetish." He jerked away from her, slipping his legs around her sides and locking his ankles behind her back, well out of her reach.

"I don't. It's just so much fun to watch you squirm."

"Well you'll just have to find something else to play with," Devin told her firmly. But he gasped in surprise when she immediately did just that.

"Ah!" she said with a wicked laugh. "I see your feet aren't your only sensitive part!"

"No," he moaned.

"No?" She stopped her playfully sensual activity.

"I mean yes! Oh, just read my mind, you little witch," he whispered hoarsely.

"I can't do that. It's probably rated X."

"So are you." He groaned as she stroked him.

The pleasure on his face was her reward. His eyes were now closed, and his hands held the sides of the tub. Bonnie anticipated his involuntary movements, exciting him to new heights. "Mmm. More to your liking, I see," she said, her voice almost a hum.

"Let's move to the bedroom," he said huskily, his thighs tightening around her, stopping her movements.

"Here is just fine," she whispered, pushing him back gently. Positioning herself astride him, she began to slip down his form. Enveloped in her warmth, Devin moaned in satisfaction, his hands reaching out to touch her face as she led him to heaven.

Lulled by the steamy heat of the water surrounding him, Devin had dozed off after their mutual labor of love. But he was awake now. "The water's getting cold," he said, hating to break the mood of the moment but feeling a distinct chill.

"Hmm. You're still warm," Bonnie mumbled, still lying on his chest, her face nuzzled in his neck. She was immensely comfortable. In her mind's eye she saw

148

herself afloat in a placid Caribbean Sea, Devin below her, the hot sun above. Or was it a dream?

"The water definitely isn't," he repeated, jostling her. She seemed to take no notice. "If you don't mind looking like a prune we could add hot water." Bonnie only snuggled closer. "That was a hint. One of us has to move to turn on the faucet," he prompted, "and you're on top, Bonnie dear."

Moving her gently to look at her face, he couldn't believe his eyes. She lay fast asleep on his chest. He stood up carefully, Bonnie in his arms. "Try *that* sometime, Superman," he said to himself as he carried her to his bed, grabbing a towel along the way. Laying her down and drying her off didn't wake her, nor did tucking her in and climbing in beside her, though she did sigh and cuddle up close.

In a final loving gesture he pulled the chopstick from her hair, allowing the flowing red waterfall to cascade across the pillows. "I'll never forgive you for falling asleep on me," he murmured. "There are so many things I wanted to tell you." His voice sounded fuzzy in his ears. In a moment he was deeply asleep himself.

CHAPTER EIGHT

There was one possible obstacle to their relationship that Bonnie had not considered: Devin might be a morning person, one of that suspicious breed who woke up immediately and cheerfully. She was not, or at least had never known herself to be, a member of that breed, and if Devin was, it could be decidedly hazardous to his health.

Bonnie's old roommate in college had been such a person, rising early in the morning full of energy and singing at the top of her lungs in the shower. Meanwhile Bonnie would crawl on her hands and knees to the kitchen for the morning infusion of hot tea, which turned her into a normal human being again. Lucky for her, that same roommate always had a cup of tea ready and waiting on the breakfast table—otherwise Bonnie would probably have strangled her.

This fine Wednesday morning, however, the sunniest in her memory, Bonnie for once got up feeling like singing herself. It was a wonderful day following a wonderful night, and she was at peace with herself, Devin, and the whole world. Of course, this miracle could have been worked by Devin's kissing her awake, or the long shower they took together—so long that the supply of hot water had nearly run out. But Bonnie knew why she felt like singing; the real magic she had waited for was truly, definitely here. She was in love.

Still full from their evening raid on the kitchen, they had tea and croissants for breakfast before going their separate ways, Devin to a full day at the clinic and Bonnie home to get ready for her full day at the shop. Once home, however, while transferring her phone back from Marcie's, she got a pleasant surprise.

Marcie's schedule had changed at the last minute, which gave Bonnie an unexpected day off. Too bad Devin had appointments all day, she thought, a warm thrill running through her at the mere thought of what they could find to do all day if he didn't. Pulling her mind resolutely back to earth, she called Megan, who was also free that day. They decided to get together to begin cleaning up some old equipment Bonnie hadn't used in quite a while.

In Bonnie's workroom they went over a large illusion on the makeshift stage. "Ever since the damned newspaper printed that article on how to saw a lady in half," Bonnie said with disgust, "this trick is pretty much useless for the stage, at least in this town. Everyone who read the story knows how it's done."

"Then why," Megan complained good-naturedly, wiping paint off her hands, "are we painting the damned thing white?"

"I figure the older children will still get a kick out of it, especially if I perform it sort of like an operation." Her expression turned thoughtful. "Maybe I'll even use you. Take you apart and put you back together again."

Megan looked less than thrilled. "Like those old comedy routines where the doctors use giant drills and saws and sledgehammers?"

"Sort of." Bonnie made a face. "You have paint on your nose. Here." She wiped it off. "My routine won't be quite so melodramatic. I want to make them laugh, not give them nightmares."

They cleaned up and had lunch while they waited for the paint to dry. "Megan, I'm curious. How did Madame Trisha compare with the others you've consulted?" Bonnie asked.

"I was wondering when we'd get back to that," she replied contritely. "The more I think about all my little trips, the more foolish I feel. Why do you ask?"

"You looked so glum when you came out of there last night. Was it because she couldn't help you find Daphne?"

Megan arched her eyebrows. "I see you had your talk with Dad."

"Yes." Among other things, she thought with a sly grin.

"Actually, I was feeling glum because I had finally come to my senses. I didn't like what I saw through skeptical eyes," Megan answered between bites of her chicken sandwich.

"How so?"

"Madame Trisha *is* different. In fact, she's downright weird. You see, all the others I've been to charge for their services. Five, ten, twenty dollars. Like that."

"For each visit? No wonder you needed a job!"

Megan smiled in forlorn amusement. "Yeah. And most of the time it takes at least five visits for them to become what they call comfortable with your presence."

Bonnie snorted derisively. "Sounds like what they're doing is making a comfortable living."

"They aren't all that comfortable taking the money, at least the majority of those I've seen. But one lady I went to—she was very sweet, by the way—was really what you'd call a fortune-teller, I suppose. Palms, tarot cards, that sort of thing. She had a set fee and collected it just like a clerk would in a shop. Even had a Better Business Bureau sticker on her wall!"

"There you go." Bonnie nodded. "I don't find that at all offensive. People can go and indulge themselves without getting hurt, as long as they aren't spending the rent money."

"Right. I remember she was very careful about things like that. Her clientele seemed to me more of a coffee klatch than anything. But some . . ." Megan's voice trailed off as she sat shaking her head.

"Some what?" Bonnie prompted.

"They wouldn't touch my money. You could put it on the table, or on a plate by the door—as you came in, of course. One rather baroque gentleman insisted you put your money in this ornate jar while he left the room. They all seemed to feel my money was tainted and would spoil their powers."

"I bet they didn't mind spending it, though," Bonnie mused. "You said Madame Trisha was different. How?"

Up to this point Megan had been explaining her

actions with some embarrassment, but now her eyes took on a hard gleam, very reminiscent of Devin's when he was angry. "I've been to her four times. The first was the night I met you. She's friendly enough, in a distant sort of way. Asks a lot of questions, but then they all do. Nothing seems to anger them more than to think you might be laughing at them, playing them along." She shuddered. "I saw a guy thrown out of one particularly tacky place once," she said.

"Did Madame Trisha ask you for money?"

"No, and that's the weird part. It's what made me think perhaps I really had found someone who could help. Now that I think about it, though, I realize I was being checked out with some higher purpose in mind. Madame Trisha was *very* interested to learn my father was a doctor."

"Who makes a lot of money," Bonnie added, nodding slowly.

"Are you thinking what I think you're thinking?" Megan asked, blue eyes sparkling with mischief.

"Do you have an appointment tonight?"

"I don't, but I can make one," Megan replied in a conspiratorial tone.

"The spirit of Harry Houdini rides again!" Bonnie cried.

Megan went to make the call. Bonnie heard just enough of the conversation to confirm her faith in Megan's ability to pull this little act off. She was a consummate actress. Returning to the kitchen wearing a big grin, Megan announced, "Madame Trisha is very anxious to see me. I have an appointment at two this afternoon."

154

"Before the banks close!" they both said together, laughing uproariously.

It turned out to be a lovely afternoon, not too hot, or at least not too hot for anyone except Madame Trisha. Megan came out ten minutes after entering the medium's house and went directly to her car, where Bonnie awaited her.

"Well?" she asked.

Megan could barely contain her excitement. "We guessed it. She said she needs spirit money. I'm supposed to bring the cash—evidently spirits don't accept checks—then ceremoniously count it in front of her, seal it in an envelope, and burn it."

"Burn it!" Bonnie exclaimed.

Megan nodded. "In this little cooker she has, looks like a miniature barbecue grill. She said it's to prove my faith to the spirits."

"You'll have to describe it to me in detail," Bonnie said absently. "How much?"

"That's the hilarious part. I asked if two hundred would be enough. She said five hundred would be a better atonement. Can you believe it!"

"I believe it," Bonnie replied with a chuckle. "How soon do our discerning spirits need the cash?"

"I told her I'd be back in an hour."

"And?" Bonnie prompted.

"Well, I sort of embellished on what you told me to tell her," Megan replied with a sly grin. "I didn't think just saying I wanted to bring a friend would go over too well, so I told her my stepmother wanted to join in the ceremony. Even that got her ire up until I man-

155

aged to convince her what a believer you are. She calmed right down."

"That's fine. As long as she accepts my presence."

Megan started the car and headed off down the street, her expression distant. "Bonnie? Do you suppose you ever will become my stepmother for real?"

"Megan!" Bonnie scolded, color rising to her cheeks. Megan's question wouldn't have bothered her if she herself hadn't been wondering the same thing just now.

"Just asking," Megan said innocently, barely suppressing a grin. A moment later she added, "Mind reading really isn't that hard, is it?"

"Drive!" Bonnie would gladly become Megan's stepmother, though she hadn't thought about it in those terms. Marrying Devin, however, she thought of constantly, especially after last night. The only trouble was, he wasn't asking. Yet.

They made a quick stop at Bonnie's bank at her insistence because it would be her skills on the line. Then they went on to the stationery store to purchase an envelope; she would have to get used to the size of the envelope with which she would practice her sleight of hand. Bonnie's last stop, at city hall, puzzled Megan, especially since it almost made them late. But they made it back to Madame Trisha's on time.

Bonnie took charge of counting out the money and putting it in the envelope. Much to Madame Trisha's consternation, she even insisted on putting it into the spiritual burner herself. But the woman checked it carefully and was satisfied, the smell of burning paper soon filling the room.

"Now the spirits will need time. Come back tomorrow evening, Megan, and I will have your answers," Madame Trisha announced solemnly.

Out in the car Bonnie produced the envelope and showed Megan the money. "Well, I'll be . . ." Megan mumbled. "I didn't see you make the switch and I was looking—hard."

"Just stick with me, sweetheart."

"Bonnie Tyson, gumshoe," Megan remarked, laughing gaily. "So what does Madame Trisha have?"

"An envelope full of newspaper. And a little surprise."

At that very moment Madame Trisha was reading her little surprise, typed on the official stationery of the district attorney and signed by him and the chief of police. Her face turned white as she read it:

> You are being watched. Your next customer may be a police officer. We would love to have you as a productive citizen of our community, preferably not as a member of our license-plate crew. You would be well advised to contact your previous clients. Be assured that *we* will be doing the same.

As Bonnie told Devin about her exploits earlier in the day, he threw his head back and laughed uproariously. They were at his house, in the kitchen, preparing the chicken they had missed the night he had set his frozen dinner on fire. Bonnie was keeping a close eye on the oven.

"So, that should bring an end to Madame Trisha's

little enterprise. She was really quite good," Bonnie said. "That paper-burner of hers was as well made as any magic prop I've ever seen."

"Maybe you could buy it from her. I have the feeling she's going to be needing the money." Devin had finished preparing the salad. "All I can say is thank you," he said, hugging her and kissing the tip of her nose. "I'm glad you could put a stop to such a heartless charlatan as Madame Trisha, or whatever her name is. But what really makes me happy is knowing this nonsense with Megan and her mediums is at an end."

Bonnie put her arms around him and hugged him back, then pushed against him playfully. "Let's not start that right now. I don't want our chicken going up in flames."

"Mmm. Let it burn," Devin murmured, nuzzling her neck. But he reluctantly released her so she could continue her vigil.

"Anyway, I don't think Megan will have the need of any more mediums. Not now," she said absently.

A frown creased Devin's brow. "What do you mean, not now?"

"I introduced her to a friend of mine. She works with the police department on occasion," Bonnie replied, prodding the chicken breasts with a fork. "These are done."

"Oh."

Bonnie was too busy putting the food on the table to notice Devin's frown. Her exciting day had given her a ravenous appetite, so she began eating hungrily. Eventually, however, she saw that Devin was barely touching his own dinner. "What's the matter? Aren't you hungry?" she asked.

"This friend of yours. Is she a detective or something?"

"Or something," she replied with a grin. Why did he look so worried? "I said she works *with* the police, not for. She's a psychic."

Devin choked on a bite of his baked potato and had to gulp his wine to wash it down. "A what!" he finally rasped.

"A psychic. Very reputable. Quite good with missing objects, even lost children. Of course, lost children usually want to be found, and it's pretty obvious Daphne doesn't. I don't pretend to know how my friend does what she does, so I don't know if that makes a difference. Still—"

"Damn!" Devin interrupted loudly. Throwing his napkin on the table, he rose angrily and walked to the window, where he looked out, blind to the beautiful sunset before him. "Why did you do a stupid thing like that?" he shot back over his shoulder.

"*Now* what have I done?" she asked in confusion, wiping her hands carefully on her napkin in an attempt to calm her own rising temper.

"Why do you insist on encouraging her?" he demanded.

Bonnie got up and went to stand next to him. "I know we have different philosophies, Devin," she began evenly, "but just because you don't believe or understand something is no reason to take it out on me, or Megan. I see nothing wrong with her attempt to find her mother through extraordinary tactics, especially since ordinary tactics have failed."

Impatiently waving her argument aside, Devin faced her with an angry expression. "That's not what I mean. I've been around you long enough now to know better than to challenge your philosophies. Megan is much the same way. You're both—"

"Pigheaded?" Bonnie supplied.

"—strong-minded," Devin finished through clenched teeth, a warning look in his eyes. "What I meant was, Why do you insist on encouraging her in this irresponsible search for Daphne?"

Eyes wide with surprise, Bonnie stared at him. "I see nothing irresponsible about trying to find a missing parent."

"She has me! And my mother and father. Don't we count?" he asked bitterly.

"Oh, Devin, of course you do!" she answered gently. "She loves you, all of you, and never misses a chance to say so. But you have to understand she feels a part of her is missing. Trying to find that missing part is natural, not irresponsible."

"It's ill-advised," he grumbled angrily.

Bonnie nodded. "That may be true," she admitted. "But face facts, Devin. She's twenty years old. This is really between her and Daphne now. The least we can do is be supportive."

"I can't believe you've done this." He glared at her. "I think it's time you left the raising of my daughter to me. This is our problem, and I'll deal with it," he said, his blue eyes as cool as an Arctic wind.

Even through the pain his words caused her, Bonnie

felt her temper flare. He had no reason to lash out at her like that. "I told you I have more than a passing interest in Megan," she shot back heatedly. "She's not just my employee, she's my friend. I want what's best for her as much as you do!"

"Oh, do you really?" he said sarcastically. "It's obvious she looks up to you. Can't you see that, by helping her this way, you're just encouraging her to continue this ridiculous waste of time?"

"Well, that's just too bad, isn't it? She's a grown woman and she'll do what she wants, no matter what either of us thinks." Bonnie tried to calm down. She barely knew what they were really fighting about! Was it Megan's obsession with finding Daphne, Bonnie's supposed interference in his daughter's life, or something else, something he was hiding from her?

There was more here than met the eye, and she was going to figure it out no matter what. "Just what are you afraid of, anyway?" Bonnie asked. "For years you let Megan go to these people who have bled her dry. Now I've introduced her to someone who just might be able to find her mother, at little or no cost, and suddenly you get upset?" She looked hard at him, seeing from the sudden uneasy expression on his face that she had hit a nerve. "Speaking of doing what's best for her, you're a little late, aren't you?"

Devin turned away from her, his fists clenched at his sides. "Damn it, Bonnie! Why couldn't you just leave well enough alone?" he demanded in anguish. "Don't you see? It was mostly my money, and I didn't care. It seemed to make Megan happy just to think she was doing something to find Daphne. But now . . ."

His voice trailed off, his hands relaxed at his sides; some inner conflict seemed finally to be at an end.

Bonnie went over to him and put her hand on his broad shoulder, feeling instinctively that she was near the truth at last, that the final piece of the puzzle was about to fall into place. "Go on," she demanded gently.

"Oh, damn! I—" He sighed heavily, turning slowly to face her. Those magnificent green eyes! He couldn't keep this from her any longer. He only hoped she would understand. "They'll take my cynic's card away from me for this," he muttered. "Now I'm afraid she might really find her mother, that this—this psychic of yours might really be able to do it. I've heard that they"—he was nearly choking on the words—"that they actually have—"

"Found missing people?" Bonnie interrupted, moved by his struggle to confess. "They have. What I don't understand is why you think it would be so bad for Megan to find Daphne?"

"Because I've already found her, that's why!" he blurted suddenly.

So stunned she could not remain standing, Bonnie dropped into a chair at the dining-room table and sat there staring at Devin, her mouth agape.

"You have to understand that when Daphne walked out on us, I considered her dead. I had no interest whatsoever in finding her. When the divorce went through, I think I'd even managed to convince myself she really *was* dead. I went through the motions when Megan asked me to, hiring a private investigator and all that. I was actually relieved when he reported she had dropped completely out of sight." Devin took a seat as well, looking very tired. "I don't really know how hard he looked. I imagine he could tell I didn't much care about finding her, and probably just went through the motions himself."

"Then how did you find her?" Bonnie asked, finally finding her tongue.

"Megan started going to mediums. Her attempts were so anguished, they tormented me night and day. I hired another detective, kept on top of him, and after quite a bit of time—and expense—he found her."

"But you didn't tell Megan," she said, trying to keep the accusation in her mind from reaching her voice. After all, she didn't know enough yet to make any judgment. All she knew was that Devin was greatly upset, and her heart went out to him. "Why?" she asked softly.

"How could I? How could I tell her that Daphne doesn't want anything to do with her past or us—ever? How do you tell your daughter that her mother couldn't care less about her, doesn't have the slightest interest in even seeing her?" he demanded with evident disgust.

Bonnie was horrified. "She said that?"

"I went and talked to her. She lives in California now, or did, and has all the fun and freedom she can stand. More than she can stand, really. I can't say it's done her any good at all, but she has it. And she can keep it," he added with grim finality.

Devin's tone was harsh, and she didn't blame him a bit. She hated Daphne, and she had never even met the woman, so she could imagine how Devin felt about her. Bonnie rose and went to stand behind his chair, she put her arms tenderly around his neck. "Devin. You have to tell her."

He stiffened. "But I just told you—"

"What Daphne said is cruel and unfeeling," Bonnie interrupted. "God! I abhor her! I find it hard to believe she even exists."

"Oh, she exists all right," Devin said acidly.

"But the fact remains that she *is* Megan's mother. Megan has a right to know. The truth may be cruel, but it's just as cruel to keep the truth from her."

"No!"

"She doesn't even know if Daphne's dead or alive. She has a right to know that at least. I think she has a right to know it all, even if it hurts. You can't keep protecting her, Devin. You have to tell her," Bonnie finished patiently, tears welling in her eyes.

Devin slammed his hand on the table. Bonnie, startled, backed away from him. "No! I can't. I won't!"

"Devin—"

"The matter isn't open for discussion," he warned, standing up and looking at her angrily.

She could see he was in pain, and she loved him more now than ever. But she was in pain too. Not because he had deceived her; his reasons for keeping his secret had been noble, if misguided. She hurt for him. She hurt for Megan too. And she hurt for herself because of what she had to say. "You have to tell her, Devin. You *have* to."

"I can't."

"I can't be a party to your deception," she said, her voice shaking with emotion. She felt as if she were

164

being torn apart, her love for Devin and his daughter on one side, her own sense of what was right and wrong on the other. Grabbing her purse, she headed for the door.

Devin caught her by the arm and swung her around. "Meaning that if I don't tell her, you will. Is that it?" he demanded furiously.

The tears that had been threatening to come finally rolled down her cheeks. "No. I'll keep your secret, for as long as it remains a secret. Megan is a bright girl, Devin. If you found Daphne, so can she, by one means or another. And when she does, it's going to hurt her far more to know you deceived her all this time—more than anything Daphne could possibly say. I'll be there for her when she needs me, because she's my friend and I love her. But I doubt I'll have much love left for the man who'll have caused her all that pain."

With a jerk she pulled away from Devin and walked out. He remained standing at the window looking after her with despair.

CHAPTER NINE

Enough was enough. Bonnie had managed to fill the four days since her argument with Devin by working at the shop, and by building some new equipment with Megan's help, all the while waiting for him to stop by or at least call. But he didn't. The days, therefore, had been bad enough, especially when she was with Megan, wanting to tell her Devin's secret and yet knowing it had to come from his lips. The nights without him were sheer hell.

Though Megan was definitely concerned over the mysterious but all-too-obvious problem her father and Bonnie seemed to be having, she held her tongue—until Monday morning when she got to the shop and found Bonnie staring intently at the phone. "I don't think that's going to work," she observed.

Bonnie looked up. "Excuse me?"

"I don't think staring at the phone will make it ring. Look," Megan said, walking over to the counter, "why don't I call him. I haven't heard from him in a while either."

"No," Bonnie replied sheepishly. "I'll do it. In a minute."

"Uh-huh."

Bonnie changed the subject: "Any luck with my psychic friend?"

"Not yet," Megan answered with a shrug. "She's nice, though. I enjoy talking with her. And she's honest. She said she'd keep trying, but the trail's pretty cold." Megan appeared lost in thought for a moment. "Do you think hiring another private detective would do any good?"

"Oh, you never know." Obviously hedging, Bonnie turned her face away from Megan's questioning gaze.

"Bonnie, what's wrong?"

Damn, Bonnie thought. This girl's getting to know me too well. How long can I keep up this charade? "Nothing! I guess I'll make that call now."

Picking up the phone, she dialed the number of the clinic and asked for Devin. Her eyes widened as she listened to the receptionist.

"I'm sorry. Dr. Warner went out of town for a few days. He should be back this afternoon. Dr. Terral is taking his patients in his absence. Do you need an appointment?"

"No, thank you," Bonnie replied, then hung up.

"Well?" Megan asked.

"He's, um, out of town. Supposed to be back this afternoon."

"Oh."

Bonnie's nonchalant tone didn't fool Megan, and Megan's sudden desire to sweep the floor didn't fool Bonnie either. They were both perturbed. Devin had left town without saying a word to either of them.

167

What was wrong with the man? How could he do this to the two people who loved him the most?

Devin was doing penance. The twelve-passenger twin-engine plane made another quick dip followed by a rapid climb, taking his stomach along for the ride. He should have known better than to grab a hamburger for lunch in Denver, which, together with the coffee he had had for breakfast in Los Angeles, sloshed threateningly in his churning stomach, adding to his already heightened sense of self-contempt. He had flown all over the map, in all kinds of aircraft and all kinds of weather, but this shuttle flight from Denver to Colorado Springs was always a nightmare of turbulence.

"Why am I such a fool?" he muttered under his breath. His white-knuckled fellow passengers took no notice. They were all busy mumbling their own epithets, most directed at the pilot or the vagaries of the air currents flowing off the Rocky Mountains. Devin leaned back in his seat and tried to relax. It would all be over soon, he reasoned grimly. One way or another.

The whole trip to California had been ill-conceived in the first place. He had thought that perhaps he could convince Daphne to at least write to Megan. He had decided to give it one more try, if only to be able to temper the bad news of his deception with the good news of a forthcoming letter or phone call. But her answer was as clear as if she had spoken it: Leave me alone. Daphne had again disappeared without a trace.

And now he was in a real quandary, the same one he had tried to escape by hopping a plane the morning after his fight with Bonnie. Telling Megan about her mother's total lack of interest would not only hurt her but reveal his deception and cause her to lose faith in him. On the other hand, if he didn't tell Megan the truth, he would lose Bonnie.

If I haven't already, he thought dismally. He had told neither Bonnie nor his daughter he was leaving, and the guilt weighed heavily on him. But he hadn't been able to face Bonnie's disapproval, and her arguments had made him realize how wrong it was not to tell Megan the truth, so he had been reluctant to talk to her as well.

But another realization had hit him, too, late at night in a lonely hotel room. Bonnie had performed her magic on his heart. Megan, his own flesh and blood, would forgive him in time, but Bonnie would never forgive his continued deceit. And a life without Bonnie seemed as impossible to him now as their relationship had seemed when they first met. Frustrating as she was at times, he had finally awakened to his love for her. He loved her and wanted her to be his forever.

It was cleaning day at the shop, and Bonnie teetered on the head step of a stepladder, still unable to reach the uppermost shelf to dust it. She had already handed down all the jars to Megan for cleaning but couldn't quite get her arm high enough to run the rag she held along the too-long-neglected surface of the shelf. "Damn!"

"Here, let me." Megan took her place and easily completed the task.

"You could at least have struggled a little," Bonnie said with playful disgust. "You didn't have to flaunt your height."

"I've just got long arms."

"That and your legs are six inches longer than mine. I think I will use you in the sawing-the-lady-in-half trick. That way I can whittle you down to size!"

They busied themselves with wiping off the jars that now lined the sales counter. "Why do you keep all the candy on the top shelf?" Megan inquired.

"So I can't reach it so easily, of course!" Bonnie replied. "Hey! I'd forgotten I had these." She unscrewed the lid of the jar she was cleaning, and popped a piece of Bavarian chocolate cream candy into her mouth, then looked sheepishly at Megan. "See what I mean?"

"No willpower," Megan said condescendingly. She looked at the expression of sheer indulgence on Bonnie's face and grabbed the jar away from her. "Give me one of those!"

Continuing to clean jars and sample the treasures within, the pair were laughing gaily when Devin walked into the shop, his face pale beneath his tan. Momentarily forgetting their mutual anger toward him, they said in unison, "You look terrible!"

Devin sighed. "Oh, good. I'd hate to think I could feel this bad on the inside and not have it show on the outside." He looked at Bonnie. "Got anything for a queasy stomach?"

Deciding now was not the time for chastisement, Bonnie nodded. "Peppermint tea usually helps." She motioned him to the back room. "Come on."

Bonnie started to prepare the tea while Devin took a seat at the table in the center of the room, but he soon stood up again.

"Excuse me," he stated, heading for the bathroom.

"Need any help?" Megan offered sympathetically.

Devin shook his head and smiled weakly. "You know the old saying. There are some things even the queen of England must do alone."

He disappeared into the bathroom and emerged a while later looking vastly improved. By his second cup of peppermint tea the color had returned to his face, and now he looked like his old self again.

"I don't know whether it was a bad hamburger or a bad plane ride," Devin explained at last. "But I feel fine now."

Good, Bonnie thought. Now she could be mad at him. "Serves you right," she said softly.

He turned to Megan, who in turn echoed Bonnie's sentiment: "I'm sorry you got sick, but don't expect much sympathy from me either."

Devin chuckled wryly. "I suppose not. I'm sorry for taking off without saying anything. I assume you found out from my receptionist?" They nodded. He sighed, and his smile disappeared. "I couldn't bear to talk to either one of you at the time, but now I'm ready. I have something to tell you, Megan."

The shop bell rang and Bonnie went to answer it, giving Devin an encouraging smile as she left the room. When she returned, he was standing beside his daughter's chair, hands in his pockets, a contrite look on his face. Megan's eyes glistened with tears, and she looked sad, but she wasn't crying. Bonnie decided Megan was a strong woman indeed.

It seemed Devin thought so too. "I must say I'm relieved to finally get this off my chest. It took awhile, but something Bonnie said finally struck home. You're not a little girl anymore. You're an adult, and a strong one. I had no right to keep on protecting you from the truth." Now he turned his eyes to the woman he loved. "Thank you, Bonnie, for helping bring me to my senses."

"You knew?" Megan asked her.

Bonnie nodded, picking up a jar full of lemon drops and wiping it absently with a cloth, clearly needing something to do with her hands. The look Devin was giving her was so warm and promising, it made her knees weak. "Yes. Your father and I had a . . . disagreement about whether to tell you or not."

"I'm glad you told me," Megan said to her father. "It hurts, but I'm relieved as well. Relieved to finally know the truth."

"There's more," Devin said. "I just got back from California. I guess I convinced myself to try one more time for your sake. What I was doing was running from the need to tell you the truth, and it didn't do me any good. Daphne's gone again. I'm afraid she's sending us a very clear message, Megan. And I think we ought to respect her wishes."

Megan nodded slowly. "Perhaps you're right, I don't know. I'd still like to get in touch with her sometime. Maybe after the hurt wears off, I'll take another stab at it." She sighed, then looked seriously at her father. "It's between her and me now, and at the moment I find myself not giving much of a damn about her either."

Devin put his hands on his daughter's shoulders, squeezing her affectionately. "I know it hurts, honey. But I have some news that may help." He looked at Bonnie, his blue eyes warmer than she had ever seen them. "You'll have a new mother soon, if she'll have me."

Bonnie's eyes widened in total surprise. "What!" She gasped.

Devin wagged a warning finger at her. "If you say you knew I was going to ask that question, so help me, Bonnie . . ." He let the threat hang in the air.

She crossed her heart, a heart that was singing with joy. "I didn't, but I do. I mean I will! Oh, Devin!" She dropped the heavy glass jar she was holding, and slid across the candy-strewn floor to the man she loved with all her heart.

He caught her and crushed her in his arms, still afraid she might disappear right before his eyes. But she didn't, and the look in her eyes as he kissed her told him she never would. "That's what I love about you," he murmured. "You're always so calm and composed."

Already starting to feel like a family, the three of them pitched in and finished the cleaning chores Bonnie had scheduled for the afternoon. After closing shop early, they went to their respective homes to change. Then Devin picked Bonnie up, and they went on to meet Megan for a celebration dinner.

The restaurant was a converted train depot, and from a table by the window they watched the trains that still ran by it as they toasted one another with wine and ate the stone-baked pizza the restaurant was famous for. Afterwards Megan said she needed to be alone for a while, so they split up and Devin drove Bonnie home. They wanted to be alone too—with each other.

"You were so right," Devin said as they sat drinking coffee in Bonnie's Victorian sitting room. "I still thought of Megan as my little girl. But she's not, is she?"

Bonnie smiled and cuddled close to him on the love seat. "In some ways she is, just as in some ways I'm still *my* father's little girl. She doesn't want that to change. She only wants you to realize that she's an adult, an individual—just as I had to convince my father too. Megan certainly proved it to you this afternoon."

"Yes. Yes, she did. No little-girl tears over being rejected, or tantrums at being overly protected. Just adult pain, and acceptance. And a strong will to continue. I'm very proud of her," Devin said firmly.

Bonnie tilted her head up from his shoulder to look into his eyes. "And I'm proud of you."

"The decision to finally tell her wasn't really that hard. I knew it would hurt her, but the alternative was far worse."

"Living a lie?"

Devin shook his head as he looked into the emerald eyes that had trapped him the moment he had first gazed into their hypnotizing depths. "Living without you. I couldn't face that," he said softly. "I love you, and living without you would be like denying a part of myself, like trying to live without my heart."

"You'll never have to." Bonnie slid her arms around his neck, her half-closed eyes drawing him closer. "I love you too. I think I lost my heart the moment I met you."

Their kiss was one of rejoicing, of quiet and profound recognition of the love they shared. With exploring tongues and deft, demanding fingers, they communicated their love with fiery touches and impassioned breathing. Devin started to pick her up in his arms to carry her to the bedroom, but she gently stilled his movements.

"It's been four days without you, my love," she whispered in his ear, playfully kissing his neck. "Even the distance to the bedroom is too far."

As her tongue delicately traced the curling patterns of his ear, Devin felt the desire within him grow in strength. "Mmm. Yes. After all, this *is* a love seat." He moaned hoarsely.

"Decadent gentleman!" she exclaimed when his hand wandered beneath her calf-length skirt.

"Decadent lady, too, I see!" His fingers nimbly unbuttoned the two buttons at her waist, allowing her skirt to unwrap and reveal lacy garments and silken hose. He soon uncovered her matching bra of see-through lace as well, his eyes smoldering with a passion that made Bonnie giddy with delight.

"Old-fashioned, perhaps, but garters have their uses," she whispered saucily.

"Indeed. Like casting spells on lovesick men." Her

bra quickly joined her skirt, his lips drawing her nipples to a tingling, throbbing hardness.

"Definitely." She gasped with pleasure. "You *do* have a fever," she remarked seductively, running her hands over his chest. "Here. Let me help cool you."

But her touch as she undressed him did anything but cool. Flames leapt within him, burning out of control. He hadn't thought it possible he could love and want Bonnie so much. If she had cast a spell on him, trapped him in the web of her magic, it was a lovely trap indeed, one from which he never wanted to escape. His lips traced an upward path along her thighs, feeling her respond to the touch of his tongue when he neared the center of her being.

Bonnie writhed beneath the loving and tender movements of his lips and gentle tongue, an urgent moan the only sound she could make. His hands reached up to cup her breasts, lovingly molding their contours. She felt as if she were being worshiped, and she was: Devin was kneeling before her in devout tribute to her femininity. Her fingernails urged him up and forward, her body becoming one with his. She could not speak, could scarcely breathe, but Devin, his open mouth covering hers, breathed life into her as the rhythm of his love swept her away.

Clinging to each other desperately, they rode the wave of their pleasure and emotion. They were in love and loving each other, their passion mixed with understanding, their desire with devotion. They were a loving couple at last, sharing their bodies and their souls. Love was the only real magic, and it surrounded them, bathed them in its fiery glow, transported them in breathless culmination.

When they could at last breathe again, Devin carried Bonnie to bed, where they cuddled each other in the gentle darkness.

"You are indeed a great magician, my love," Devin whispered softly.

"So are you, my love." Bonnie sighed. "So are you."

CHAPTER TEN

At the altar of the little chapel, surrounded by a small group of friends, his own and Bonnie's, Devin stood gazing down the aisle apprehensively. Not all his nervousness was wedding-day jitters. At the other end of the aisle, behind closed double doors, were the original Mysterious Tyson and his daughter. Anything could happen—and probably would. Bonnie's mother beamed at him from the front pew, her green eyes even more penetrating than her daughter's, if that was possible.

As Devin watched in amused horror, the doors swung open and the elder Tyson wheeled in a six-foot-tall cabinet. He was a striking man—and especially so in his black tuxedo—with a magnificent head of white hair. The tips of his white mustache were waxed into dramatic points. Gray eyes twinkling, he opened the cabinet front and back so the onlookers could see straight through. It was empty. He quietly walked around and through it, tapping the sides as he moved, then he closed the doors and spun it around once. When he opened the cabinet again, Bonnie stepped out, looking stunningly beautiful in a long, white silk gown, her hair flowing free beneath a small veil. Everyone gasped, including the bemused minister.

As a performer, Bonnie had always loved being the center of attention, and she certainly was that now. All her friends and Devin's, all the relatives from both sides, were watching her. Even her friend Amy Tanner and Amy's husband, Cole, had managed to come this afternoon, back early from their vacation because of Amy's advanced pregnancy. Originally Amy was supposed to be Bonnie's maid of honor, but she was so heavy with child she decided it would be best to watch instead of participate. Tears of happiness streamed down her radiant face.

Bonnie took her father's arm and glided up the aisle to Devin. Winking at her husband-to-be, she moved her hands and a lovely bouquet of flowers appeared in them. She looked at him mischievously. He looked heavenward. The ceremony commenced.

When the minister asked for the ring, a blank expression came over Devin's face as he started patting his pockets, looking at his fingers—at anything he could think of. "Oh, no," he muttered.

Megan reached her hand across to him, palm up and empty. Making a fist, she passed her other hand over it, and when she opened her clenched hand the ring Devin and Bonnie had picked out three weeks earlier was there, sparkling at him. He gave his daughter a baleful glance and handed the ring to the chuckling minister.

The remainder of the ceremony was, in Devin's opinion, blessedly uneventful. He kissed his new bride, they posed for a few pictures, then, amid a shower of rice, it was off to the reception in a chauffeur-driven limousine. Devin tried not to think about the fact that most of the rice seemed to be coming from the direction of the Tysons, though neither of them lifted a hand to throw any. It was not only overwhelming to have so many magicians in the family, he decided, it was downright spooky. They drove away from the church preceded by a cloud of smoke.

"That's the first wedding I've been to where there was more applause than there were tears," Devin commented with a sigh. One look at Bonnie's smiling face, however, and suddenly everything ceased to matter—everything except the happiness they shared. "I love you, Mrs. Warner," he said softly.

"And I love you, Mr. Warner." Her radiant face turned thoughtful. "The Mysterious Tyson-Warner." she muttered.

"Oh, no," Devin said.

"The Mysterious Warner?"

He made a face. "Shut up and kiss me," Devin replied, pulling her close and ignoring the obvious interest of the chauffeur.

Devin didn't know how calm the wedding had been until he compared it with the reception. It started off with a flurry of excitement when Amy Tanner had to leave.

"Are you all right?" Bonnie asked.

"I'll be fine. Probably just a false alarm," Amy replied. "Nothing to—ouch!—worry about." The Tanners departed hastily, Amy leaning on Cole, who looked white as a sheet.

There were a lot of show people from Bonnie's side

present, and although her other friends were used to them, Devin's staid professional acquaintances were not. Still, everyone was having a good time, particularly Devin's mother and father, who took an immediate shine to the Tysons.

"My mom and dad are really getting along well with yours, don't you think?" Bonnie asked, devouring her third piece of wedding cake.

"Hmm. Your dad's teaching mine card tricks. I have the feeling mine'll get arrested at his next Saturday-night poker game." He reached out and wiped a bit of frosting from the corner of Bonnie's mouth. "Don't you go and get fat on me!"

She hugged him close, moving against him with a subtle sensuality. "I think I'll be getting enough exercise later to burn these calories off."

"You're right," he replied huskily. "You will." Devin looked around the room. "What say we take off right now?"

"Well . . ." she hedged, obviously tempted.

"Nobody will miss us," he coaxed.

Bonnie observed the party, deciding he was right. Marcie had succumbed to the charms of an investment banker friend of Bonnie's father, and was talking to him animatedly in a corner of the gaily decorated banquet room. Megan seemed equally absorbed in conversation with one of Devin's younger partners from the clinic, but they were doing their talking on the small dance floor. In fact, everyone was involved in one form of festive activity or another, from drinking champagne and attacking the lavish buffet to gathering around Bonnie's mother, who regaled her enthralled listeners with tales of Irish demons and Tibetan banshees.

Although they tried to slip away without being seen, one person in the throng did catch them—the Mysterious Tyson himself. "Leaving so soon?" he inquired, startling them when he appeared in the path of their escape route down the outside hallway.

"Father!" Bonnie gasped. "We—we thought you were still . . ."

"I didn't teach you *everything* I know, my child," he answered, his gray eyes dancing with mischief. He came up to them, taking one of their hands in each of his and squeezing warmly. "Your mother, in her equally mysterious way, says there will be children in the future for you two. So," he said with a wink, "I won't keep you. Just know we all love you, and wish you all the best the world has to offer—which is a great deal if you take the time to enjoy it." Pressing their hands together, he smiled enigmatically, snapped his fingers, and presented Bonnie with the largest white rose she had ever seen. By the time they had looked from the flower back to him, he had gone.

"How does he *do* that?" Devin asked of her father's ability to come and go without being seen. It was a habit that had disconcerted Devin more than once in the week her parents had been in town. Bonnie started to speak, but he cut her off. "Yes, I know, don't tell me. He does it very well."

Laughing and holding hands, they went down the hotel corridor and out to the car. Only there did they try to separate, and notice something was wrong. The

Mysterious Tyson senior had handcuffed them together.

Bonnie started laughing uncontrollably. Devin simply pursed his lips and read the note dangling from the center link of the stainless-steel restraints. "Now you are *really* married. Enjoy!"

"That's my dad!" Bonnie exclaimed proudly, setting her rose down on the fender of the car so she could get a better look at the handcuffs.

"Very funny," Devin said with dry humor. "Do your thing and get us out of these. People are starting to stare."

Bonnie looked up and noticed that a couple, who had just emerged from a blue Mercedes, were giving them covert glances as they crossed the parking lot. She raised her arm and waved—Devin's hand naturally following, as it was linked to hers—and gave them a big smile. "Desperate criminal here. Have to haul him in for questioning." The couple looked away and hurried into the hotel.

Muttering under his breath, Devin unlocked the driver's door and prodded Bonnie until she climbed inside, sliding across the seat to make room for him. "Will you hurry up and pick the lock or something?" he demanded once they were in the car and away from curious eyes.

Bonnie studied the handcuffs. "Oh, no!" she yelped.

"What?" Devin asked impatiently. He was getting an uneasy feeling, brought about by the expression of shock on Bonnie's face.

"He had these made!"

"So?"

"So there isn't any lock to pick, or at least no way to get at the mechanism."

"Well, do something! Anything!"

Bonnie worked her wrist against the unyielding steel, using all the tricks she knew. "It's no use. We'll have to cut them off," she announced at last.

"Oh, Lord." Devin gave an exasperated sigh.

"What's the matter?" she asked, pouting sensually. "You don't like the idea of being trapped with me the rest of the night?"

Devin shook his head and laughed. "I don't mind one bit. It'll just make things difficult, that's all." He raised his eyebrows. "Consider the fact that we'll have to take a shower with your gown and my shirt dangling in the middle of the chain."

She hadn't thought of that. Other things came to mind as well. "Do something!"

"There's a locksmith about a block away. They should have the tools to cut us out of these. Or you could just say the magic word and—"

"I'll give *you* a magic word!" Bonnie cried, suddenly feeling panicky. "Drive!"

But once again Devin's car had other ideas. It wouldn't start. Together—there was no other way—they hurried to the locksmith, trying to look as inconspicuous as possible.

Not inconspicuous enough, however. A policewoman on foot patrol couldn't help but notice the man in a tuxedo and the woman in a white wedding gown almost running down the sidewalk toward her. "Aren't you two a bit old for punk fashion?" she

184

asked, looking askance at the handcuffs they were unsuccessfully trying to hide.

After some frantic explanation they were allowed to continue on, accompanied by the patrolwoman who chuckled every step of the way. Equally amused was the locksmith, an elderly woman who laughed the whole time she worked at cutting the handcuffs off. Afterwards Devin called a cab and they finally made it home, embarrassed but still full of anticipation for the evening ahead of them.

Bonnie's house was home for them now. Devin had always felt at ease here in her miniature castle with its unusual, dramatic decor and so had decided to let Megan take up residence at his place.

"I've just realized something," Devin said as they sipped champagne on the patio, enjoying the sunset. "You've been on your best behavior, haven't you?"

Bonnie looked at him with wide-eyed innocence. "Whatever do you mean?"

"I mean I just figured out what I've gotten myself into," he replied. "Everything's relatively normal until my wedding day. Then my bride appears from nowhere, my daughter produces your wedding ring from thin air, and your father handcuffs us together. I think I'm in trouble," he concluded, sighing in mock resignation.

"I'll admit I've been taking it easy on you," she said, her eyes full of mischief. "But I've got you now! Unless," she added slyly, "you've decided to back out?"

Grinning, Devin got up from his chair, pulling Bonnie to her feet as well. He put his arms around her and locked his hands at the small of her back. "You remember that fantasy I told you I had, the night we first had dinner here?"

"Mmm." Bonnie reveled in the feel of his warm body pressed against hers. "You never did tell me what it was."

"I'm living it, right now," he explained, kissing her hair softly. "To be here, with you, to know you're mine. I may have to look out for my ears, and be extra careful whenever your parents come to visit, but that's okay. I've got you now, too, and the only way you'll get rid of me is to make me disappear." He pulled her tighter against his hips, his mouth devouring hers with a desperate hunger.

"Never. I much prefer you here, in the flesh," Bonnie murmured happily.

"Now that's the kind of disappearing act I had in mind." Devin swept her into his arms and carried her inside.

"Put me down, you brute!" she teased. "I have a couple of things to attend to first."

He set her down. "Very well. But if you aren't back in this bedroom in five minutes, I'll come looking for you," he promised with gruff sensuality.

She was back in three, waiting on the bed for him when he stepped out of the bathroom. Bonnie looked up at her new husband from where she lay, arms stretched out in invitation. She wore only a seductive bit of lace. Her emerald eyes smoldered as she watched Devin's strong, lean form.

"Now you're going to ask me if I've disconnected

186

the phone," Bonnie announced in a playful, mysterious tone of voice.

"Mmm," Devin murmured as he joined her on the bed, his lips trailing along her smooth thigh.

"And if I've locked and bolted the door."

He didn't answer. He was too busy loosening the already tenuous hold of the filmy wisp of lace on her shoulder.

She gasped as his teeth bit gently at her neck. "And, yes, I remembered to have Marcie and Megan swap phone numbers in case anything happens at the shop, and . . ." Bonnie's voice trailed off, and a strange gleam came to her eyes.

Devin looked at her face and sighed in exasperation. "I know that expression. What's wrong now?"

"I—I don't know," she answered, a frown creasing her brow. "I won't be a moment," she added, getting up hurriedly and going to the phone in the next room.

Devin watched her delicious body disappear through the doorway, counted patiently to ten, then stomped after her. "Bonnie, I'm going to—"

She held up her hand excitedly. "That's fantastic! Thank you so much for calling!" she said, then hung up the phone.

Devin looked at her warily. "Now what!"

"Amy's just had a baby boy! We have to go—" She stopped, watching Devin's face curiously. "What are you doing?"

He had placed his fingers on his temples, his eyes closed in apparent concentration. "I'm getting a mental image."

"Oh, Devin!" She laughed.

187

"It's becoming clearer. Yes. I see it all now."

Still laughing at his outrageous behavior, Bonnie prompted him playfully. "Okay. What do you see?"

"I see . . . I see a man. Yes, a very frustrated man," he announced dramatically. He slowly opened his eyes, fixing her with a gleaming stare of his own. "And if that man's wife doesn't come back to bed right now, I foresee terrible things happening to her!" With that he lunged forward and grabbed her, ignoring her squeal of protest as he threw her over his shoulder and carried her to the bedroom.

"But what about Amy and the baby?" Things were happening to her, all right, but they were far from terrible. Only Devin knew how to do the kind of magic he was performing on her now. She gasped with pleasure, her heartbeat flying.

"You can see them later, during visiting hours. Give me half a chance," he whispered sensually in her ear, "and you'll be seeing plenty of babies."

"I—I will?" she said, her voice catching in her throat. Bonnie wasn't struggling now. She gave in totally, and gladly, to the waves of pleasure flowing over and through her. "H—how?" she teased.

Devin chuckled wickedly. "Magic!" he whispered. "The oldest and best magic of them all."

All-new

Candlelight Newsletter

An exceptional, *free* offer awaits readers of Dell's incomparable Candlelight Ecstasy and Supreme Romances.

Subscribe to our all-new CANDLELIGHT NEWSLETTER and you will receive—at absolutely no cost to you—exciting, exclusive information about today's finest romance novels and novelists. You'll be part of a select group to receive sneak previews of upcoming Candlelight Romances, well in advance of publication.

You'll also go behind the scenes to "meet" our Ecstasy and Supreme authors, learning firsthand where they get their ideas and how they made it to the top. News of author appearances and events will be detailed, as well. And contributions from the Candlelight editor will give you the inside scoop on how she makes her decisions about what to publish—and how *you* can try your hand at writing an Ecstasy or Supreme.

You'll find all this and more in Dell's CANDLELIGHT NEWSLETTER. And best of all, *it costs you nothing.* That's right! It's Dell's way of thanking our loyal Candlelight readers and of adding another dimension to your reading enjoyment.

Just fill out the coupon below, return it to us, and look forward to receiving the first of many CANDLELIGHT NEWS-LETTERS—overflowing with the kind of excitement that only enhances our romances!

Candlelight
Ecstasy Romances™

$1.95 each

At your local bookstore or use this handy coupon for ordering:

DELL READERS SERVICE—Dept B581C
P.O. BOX 1000. PINE BROOK. N.J. 07058

Please send me the above title(s). I am enclosing $_____ (please add 75¢ per copy to cover
postage and handling). Send check or money order—no cash or CODs. Please allow 3-4 weeks for shipment.
CANADIAN ORDERS: please submit in U.S. dollars.

Ms./Mrs./Mr._____

Address_____

City/State_____ Zip_____

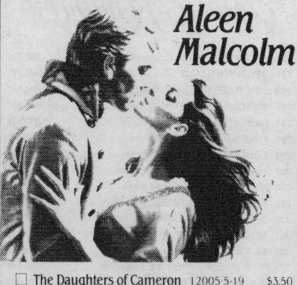